D1559910

THE COMMITTED SIDE CHICK

TINA MARIE

Cole Hart
SIGNATURE NOVELS

The Committed Side Chick

Copyright © 2020 by Tina Marie

All rights reserved.

Published in the United States of America.

All rights reserved. No part of this publication may be reproduced, distributed, or transmitted in any form or by any means, including photocopying, recording, or other electronic or mechanical methods, without the prior written permission of the publisher, except in the case of brief quotations embodied in critical reviews and certain other noncommercial uses permitted by copyright law. For permission requests, please contact: www.colehartsignature.com

This is a work of fiction. Names, characters, places, and incidents either are the products of the author's imagination or are used fictitiously. Any resemblance of actual persons, living or dead, businesses, companies, events, or locales is entirely coincidental. The publisher does not have any control and does not assume any responsibility for author or third-party websites or their content.

The unauthorized reproduction or distribution of this copyrighted work is a crime punishable by law. No part of the book may be scanned, uploaded to or downloaded from file sharing sites, or distributed in any other way via the Internet or any other means, electronic, or print, without the publisher's permission. Criminal copyright infringement, including infringement without monetary gain, is investigated by the FBI and is punishable by up to five years in federal prison and a fine of $250,000 (www.fbi.gov/ipr/).

This book is licensed for your personal enjoyment only. Thank you for respecting the author's work.

Published by Cole Hart Signature, LLC.

Mailing List

To stay up to date on new releases, plus get information on contests, sneak peeks, and more,

Go To The Website Below...

www.colehartsignature.com

TEXT TO JOIN

To stay up to date on new releases, plus get exclusive information on contests, sneak peeks, and more...

Text ColeHartSig to (855)231-5230

ACKNOWLEDGMENTS

I would first like to thank God for giving me this gift of writing and for providing me with every blessing I have received this far and will receive in the future.

I want to thank my family, my fiancé, Jay, for putting up with all the late nights and my crazy moods while I am writing. To my kids: Jashanti, Jaymarni and Jasheer, I want you to know that I work so hard so you can have it all.

To my Cole Hart Presents team, salute to all of you for keeping on the grind and staying positive. Cole, the fact that you wanted me on your team means more to me than you will ever know. Princess, and Anna I swear you ladies are just amazing and I love you! Twyla, there is no category for someone like you, any time I need a shoulder, a friend or a talking to you are there. I know you sick of me but I'mma love you foreverrrrr! Jammie and Reese, you two truly just make my life complete, and I thank God for giving me friends like you. I want to thank all of my Pen Sisters no matter what company you are in for all of the love, support and for always helping to push me to my next goal. I appreciate you all!

Ladora, you are the world's best little sister. I love you, and I believe in you always!

Natasha, we have been friends for what seems like forever, and now you're more like family. You could never be replaced in my life. You have seen me at my best and worst and still have my back. Oh, and you have learned to put up with all my moods. LOL. I love you, boo!

Natavia, only in a perfect world would I have thought that my favorite author would be my real-life friend. And even though this isn't a perfect world, I am so happy you became my friend. I value all the talks, laughs, wcc and advice. Love you soul sister (inside joke).

Coco, I didn't think I could write a dedication to you without crying—I was right. You are a bomb a*** little sister. I would go to war for you with anyone. The way you love on my son and have never turned your back on me is everything. You're filled with positivity and joy, and I can't find the words to thank you. I love you!

Sunni there are so many days you have talked me off the ledge and just been a friend I love your whole life. I could never replace you. Your bestseller is right around the corner. I can feel it!

Nisey, Quanisha and Keke you three have been rocking with me since forever and are the best admins ever. I love how you love me but most of all, how you all have come to love each other. Tina, you may be new to the team, but you are a welcome addition! You ladies don't let me forget a thing and handle all the grunt work, so I can write. XoXo! To my test readers, Kristi, Sweets and Jammie, there would be no book without you ladies, you all are my blessings! Tootie and Liz I couldn't ask for better promoters- one thing I learned in this business is it takes a team and finding the two of you completed my team.

To my Baby Momma Zatasha, even though we are both crazy Gemini's I still love you boo. Couldn't do this book ish without you!! And to all the Bookies, I appreciate the love and support you show all authors, not just me. It makes a difference having a place where we are respected, celebrated and offered endless support!

To my friends and family: I appreciate all of the love and support. My cousins, Claire, Dionne, Donna & Tanisha. My friends: Letitia, Natasha, Jennifer, Sharome, Shante, Diana and Kia. I'm truly grateful for you all, and I love you. To my best friend, there will never be enough letters in the alphabet to thank you for everything, so I won't even try.

To all of my fans, readers, test readers, admins and anyone who has ever read or purchased my work, shared a link or a book cover, you're all appreciated, and I promise to keep pushing on your behalf to write what you're looking for.

🎜 I 🎝

ARABELLA

BACK IN THE DAY

Stepping out of the shower, the house had an eerie silence that made my skin crawl. I grabbed my towel and wiped the steam from the mirror. As soon as I did, I saw him standing behind me. I jumped, and he laughed as he snatched my towel and spun me around. "My sweet girl is all grown up now," Alex sneered, his eyes filled with lust. I backed up as much as I could until the back of my knees hit the tub. Right before I could fall in, he grabbed my arms and snatched me close to his body.

I knew this day would come, but I thought I had more time. Twenty-four hours more to be exact. I thought about fighting him, kicking him in his nuts and running, but running where? I was still in high school. I had no job or money, and this was my mom's house. Alex pinched my nipple, causing me to cry out. "Seventeen will get you thirty," my sister sang from the doorway. Her face was blank, but her tone of voice was amused. I prayed that I didn't become so damaged in this household that shit like this would become a joke to me one day.

His hand fell, and he frowned deeply. I didn't know if my sister just saved me or made shit worse. Alex was unpredictable and judging by today's nonsense, he no longer cared who knew that he wanted his girlfriend's kids. Slowly he backed away before grinning down at me. "Well, since I have to wait a little longer for my first taste and since you have inserted yourself into my business, Keke you will just have to do for now. But Bella, I will see you soon." He grabbed Keke's arm after he winked at me, then he left the bathroom. I stood there shaking, tears racing down my cheeks as I listened to the sex sounds from my sister's bedroom. Picking up my towel, I crept to my room to get dressed for my last night of freedom.

✦

"COME ON BELLA, if I'm going to get you in this club, we have to hurry the fuck up," my sister Keke fussed as I just stood there. I kept looking in the mirror at my reflection. I didn't even look like myself. The weave my sister installed in my hair fell to both sides of my face, the waves rippling in the dim lamp light. I rarely wore make-up, but tonight I decided to do a natural look, one I learned on the fly from a YouTube video.

"It's not too late for you to wear the dress I bought you," Keke said standing behind me holding the sheer black scrap of cloth in her hands. I just shook my head. I knew my sister was pissed at my choice of outfit, but tonight was about me. It was my last night before I would become a victim, Alex's victim and I was going to do whatever the fuck I wanted. Besides, I liked the look of my ripped white-washed blue jeans, red lace corset and red satin heels. It was sexy but classy.

"No offense but I don't want to look like a hoe," I responded. I glanced at her too short white dress. It was so tight I could see that she had on no panties and her brown nipples poked through the fabric. I wished she would at least wear a bra. Shaking my head, I grabbed my black MK wristlet and headed to my bedroom door, indicating I was ready.

"Bella, you act like you not about to go do some hoe shit." She rolled her eyes and threw the dress on my bed.

"And you act like this hoe shit wasn't your suggestion. I can't be too much of a hoe because I'm still a virgin," I barked back. I thought about just staying home since Keke was being a pain in my ass and I doubted I could even go through with the plan. But thoughts of being home alone with Alex had me changing my mind.

Neither one of us said another word as we climbed in the white Nissan Altima that my sister was driving. I wondered what nigga she was fucking this time that let her use his car. Ever since Alex broke her in, she was bussing it open for every dude that looked her way. Maybe she was looking for love in all the wrong places or some shit. But no matter what Alex did to me I swear I wasn't going down that road. "Now remember, you don't have to find anyone on your own. I got some potential men already lined up. I will bring them over, introduce you and once you find one you like I will let him know what's up."

I gave Keke the side-eye, this shit was beginning to feel like she was pimping me out. I let her talk me into losing my virginity before Alex could take it. But the whole point was that whoever I chose to be my first would be someone I was interested in. Not her. I didn't respond, just watched the light rain outside my window until we pulled up in front of club Point. I had been to a few house parties but nothing like this. Half-naked girls were standing in a line that damn near wrapped around the building. I was assuming the free before midnight for ladies was the reason.

A group of men walked towards the door, and everyone stopped to look. They had their hoods up like they were about to rob the place instead of coming to the party. But the amount of ice they had on let me know that wasn't even necessary. They stopped for the bouncer as he lifted the red velvet rope to let them in. That was when I saw him, he turned to check out his surroundings, and for a second his honey-colored brown eyes met mine. His facial expression was blank, so I couldn't tell what he was thinking. Then suddenly, he disappeared inside. "Hello, I've been talking to you," Keke snapped breaking me from my thoughts.

I focused my eyes on her so she could see I was listening. Raising one of my eyebrows, I waited. Keke parked in the lot across the street. Turning my way, she grabbed my hand. "I know it seems like I'm forcing you into this. But I'm just trying to protect you. Having Alex break my virginity still haunts me. Had I known how horrific the experience with Alex was going to be, I would have gone and had sex with anyone else, even one of the crackheads from the corner store. Alex got a thrill from taking my virginity and hurting me in the process, and he is looking to do the same thing with you." She tightened the grip on my hand, and a tear raced down her cheek. "So please, Bella, let someone, anyone else be your first. Because in a few hours you will be eighteen and Alex will be waiting."

"Ok," I said almost in a whisper as we got out. We made our way to the same entrance the guy with the honey-colored eyes went through and stopped at the rope. I could see females glaring at me, some rolling their eyes and popping slick shit. A few minutes later, some guy in a True Religion fit and fresh out the box Jordan's nodded to the bouncer. The rope was lifted, and we were waved inside. I watched as my sister smiled in the guy's face, she ran her hand over his dreads, all the way down to the front of his jeans. He slapped her on the ass and looked at her with nothing but lust. There was something about him that turned me off, I didn't know if it was the fact that he had on so much jewelry. Like this nigga was rocking ten chains, rings on every finger and on both hands, and as a finale, a dull ass gold tooth on the top and bottom of his mouth. He was trying way too fucking hard. Or maybe it was the way his sneaky eyes roamed around the club looking every female up and down, including me. He reminded me of Alex.

"Tim, this is my sister I was telling you about, Bella. Bella this is my boo, Tim," Keke introduced us all smiles and shit. I gave a little uncomfortable wave and trailed behind them to a small table across from the bar. All his homeboys looked as tacky as him, and sadly a few looked interested in me. I would run up out this bitch now if Keke thought I was giving myself to these niggas. I was about to enjoy myself tonight, and I would deal with whatever else tomorrow, whether I was a virgin or not.

"Sis, I'm about to go to the bar and grab a drink. I will be back." She nodded as she popped a pill that Tim handed her and downed it with a cup of some dark liquid. I just shook my head. I felt like I barely knew Keke these days. I went to stand at the bar and prayed I didn't get asked for ID. After waiting a few minutes, finally, it was my turn, but instead of taking my order, the bartender smiled wide as hell and spoke to someone behind me. My head whipped around to see who the fuck was cutting in front of me. Looking up it was the same guy who I was enthralled with earlier. He already had a drink in his hand, so I had no idea why the fuck she was entertaining him before me.

"Yo, tell that bitch Stacy she forgot the fucking Ace of Spades. I shouldn't even have to come down here." I could tell he was pissed by the scowl on his face. He turned to leave but not before bumping me and spilling his liquor down the front of my corset. Before I could cuss his ass out, I felt his hand brush my breasts as he followed the trail of the sticky liquid. "My bad shorty," he said, leaning closer to me. I could smell his alluring cologne, and I felt my pussy throb. Shit, I barely knew how to work this bitch and she was ready to hop on his dick.

"It's cool," I said stuttering a little. His presence had my head spinning.

"I can replace ya shit, how much?" His deep voice had me wishing he would talk to me all day. I wondered if I could take that in payment.

I shook my head laughing. "What the hell kind of females you be used to? It can wash, it will survive to see another day."

He gave me a half-smile causing a dimple to appear on his right cheek. "Aight, well you be good ma." He removed his hand, and I felt like I was a baby, and someone snatched my blankie. "Yo Gina, her drinks on me," he shouted to the bartender who ignored me in the first place. He gave her a look, and she stopped talking to the person she was serving and stood patiently waiting on my order.

"I will have a sex on the beach," I said. Before I could thank him, I looked back, and he was gone. I made it a point to find out where he went and I spent the next two hours watching his sexy ass upstairs in the VIP. He was sitting back on the red leather couch drinking straight from the bottle. I watched girl after girl throw themselves at him, but he didn't seem impressed. That made me like him more.

"Hey wassup wit you," one of Tim's homeboys said as he slid next to me.

"Hey," I replied dry as fuck. His hand caressed my arm, and I moved ten steps to the right. I looked back upstairs at the man I wished I was standing next to and I realized he was watching me. Smirking, he winked at me before focusing on the female who was basically giving him a lap dance.

"Really Bella, Greg was trying to holla at you," Keke hissed in my ear. "He is the one, so you need to be getting to know him instead of acting like a stuck-up bitch." My eyes widened in shock at everything she had just said. The nigga she thought I was fucking for the first time looked like an undercover junkie. His haircut was leaned to the side like he did that shit himself and got tired in the middle, and his barely clean white shirt smelled like funk. Not to mention I was still getting over the fact that my sister just called me a bitch because of his ass.

"Keke, calm down, I found the one I'm going home with tonight. And it sure as fuck isn't him," I said grilling Greg.

"Who, then?"

"Him," I replied nodding my head in the direction of the mystery man. I didn't know what I expected, but her laughter wasn't it.

"Girl hell naw, do you know who that is? That's Sire, one of the not nice crew. First off, those niggas are crazy as fuck. Second, he's a boss ass nigga, and I'm sure he isn't out here looking to pop some little girl's cherry. Now if you don't like Greg, what about Petey? He is Tim's cousin and kind of cute." I felt my chest cave in with disappointment as she pointed to a guy who was way better than Greg but had the creepy rapist vibe of Tim.

I just shrugged. I was still trying my hand at Sire before the night was over. I sipped my drink and danced to the music playing. The DJ was hitting, so I had no problem feeling the beat. The night came to an end, and after three strong ass drinks, I was buzzed. Making my way to the door, somehow, I lost sight of Sire. Keke was gripping my arm as we hit the sidewalk, like she was scared that I was going to flee. Disappointed, I followed behind her like a sheep going to slaughter.

I smelled him before I could see him. It was like I felt his presence near me. Slowly I snatched my arm from my sister and turned to face him. "Hey," I said causing him to stop walking and look down at me. I wondered how tall he was, at least six foot two, I loved the way he towered over me.

"What's good lil mama?"

"Umm, first of all, I wanted to thank you for the drinks." He nodded and stood there waiting on me to say something else. I just knew I was fucking this up. Keke was standing off to the side with Tim and Petey, her eyes narrowed into evil slits. I guess I was fucking up her plan, but I didn't care. Finding my courage, I decided to just go for it. "And second, I'm trying to leave wit you, so you tell me what's good." I couldn't believe I basically just asked some man to leave a club with me and fuck.

I could see amusement in his eyes as he took his big hand and lifted my chin some, so I was looking right at him. "Nah shorty, I'm good, you not even ready for a nigga like me." He let me go and walked away.

"I told ya slow ass he wasn't fucking wit you," my sister hissed in my ear as she damn near drug me to the car. Tim stood there rubbing his hands together as he watched. Stopping suddenly causing her to damn near drop on the ground. I was having second thoughts on going anywhere with them.

SIRE

I WATCHED lil mama as she walked with her people, a girl who resembled her and wanna be a gangster ass Tim and Petey. I had seen the girl with her around before, her ass was thirtsy, always tryig to spread her pussy around for a come up. Petey let his hand grip shorty's waist, and for some reason I was pissed. "Son, the fuck you over here looking mad for. She asked was you taking her back to the hotel to fuck, and you turned her down. Now let the homies get some." My cousin Cahir stopped long enough to talk shit before he grabbed two bitches and made his way to valet. That nigga was wild as fuck, I couldn't do anything but shake my head at him.

My brother Remee snickered as he stood next to me. "Let me find out you checking for that little young girl. She do got a fat ass," he said, causing his girlfriend Rumor to punch him in the side. "I'm just saying babe, for him, not me." He laughed as they walked off leaving me standing there with my thoughts. I only turned shorty down because she looked like a good girl. She sho as fuck wasn't ugly, when I spilled my drink on her earlier just looking at her pretty ass had my dick hard. Her laugh was everything, and so was the fact that she passed up the money I offered to replace her shirt. She gave me wifey vibes if I was looking to settle down. But I wasn't.

I looked back one more time as she was damn near being pushed into the backseat of a Nissan by the girl and Petey. He was fondling her breasts at the same time, and baby girl looked disgusted. She had one hand on the top of the car and the other she used to try and slap his hand away, but he was stronger than her. The way Tim stood back licking his lips as he looked on, had me feeling like this shit was some kind of a set up. Shorty looked up and caught my eye, and all I saw was terror, that shit had me moving her way.

"Yo Pete, lil mama coming wit me." I damn sure wasn't calling no grown ass man Petey. He grilled me. "No disrespect Sire but this is my bitch now and she ain't going wit you." Her eyes got wide when she heard that, and she snatched her arm from his grip. Only for him to grab her shit hard enough for her to cry out.

I didn't even think about it, I bawled my hand into a fist and damn near knocked Petey's head off. Grabbing lil mama she melted into my body, her arms wrapped around my waist as she held on like a scared child. Petey was holding his face as blood dripped onto the ground. I made sure I had my hand near my gun in case him or his pussy ass cousin tried to jump bad. But I knew my name made niggas shake in these streets, so I didn't expect it.

"Really Bella, you bout to go with him? This nigga doesn't want nothing but to fuck. You don't want to go out like a hoe. Petey is trying to be ya fucking man and you just straight disrespecting him," her people begged as we turned to leave. She had tears in her eyes as Tim had her by the back of the neck. He manhandled her for a minute before shoving her in the car. Yea some shit wasn't right here at all. Tim thought him and his cousin were about to be running through lil mama tonight. But that shit was dead now. We made it to my whip, and I helped her in the passenger seat.

She looked over and gave me a grateful smile as soon as I sat down.

"Thank you," she damn near whispered.

"It's all good Bella. Your homegirl is shady as fuck though, you really need to be more careful who you hanging out wit."

"That was my sister," she said looking out the window at the car her sister was thrown into by Tim.

"Damn ma, that's fucked up." I didn't really know what else to say. I only had one sister, and this was why I made sure her ass stayed in the house. I grabbed her hand for a minute and caressed her soft skin. Hitting the push to start, I had to think where the fuck I was taking her. I didn't book a hotel room because honestly, I had no plans on bringing any bitches home with me tonight. Pulling off I was about to do some shit I made a rule not to, I was taking Bella to my crib.

"Arabella is my name actually. But you can call me Bella." She smiled again, and I damn near ran off the road watching her pretty ass.

"Shit I'm being rude as fuck, I'm Sire," I said.

"I know, I was already put up on who you were, and how you would never fuck with a girl like me." She smirked, but I could tell that she was insecure because of whoever told her that bullshit. I didn't comment, but for some reason it had me mad as fuck. I bet it was her hating ass sister. That thirsty bitch stayed trying to put my dick on her lips every time she saw me, and I stayed turning her down. It only took me twenty minutes to get to my house from the club, the whole ride there I made sure no one was following me just in case. I was a young rich nigga so I could never be too careful. Parking in my garage I looked over and noticed shorty was half asleep. Damn, I didn't even know what the fuck I was doing wit her right now.

"Come on ma, we're here." She sat up and opened her own door. She didn't look around much when we stepped inside, but I did notice her eyes light up when she saw my state-of-the-art kitchen. It would have been nice to have lil mama cook me a meal, except I ain't have shit in here to cook. There was nothing here really besides some cereal and tuna fish. I led her to the couch and got a bottled water for both of us. "You good?"

"Yea, I umm didn't expect this," she said her arm sweeping the room. "I mean for you to bring me to your house and all." Damn, was she the type of girl who been hopping on nigga's dicks in hotel rooms every night of the week? Just because she looked innocent and I hadn't seen her ass before didn't mean she wasn't of the thot persuasion. You never could tell with these females and her sister was definitely one.

"Yea I can see this being a surprise, shit it was a surprise for me too. But you seem like you worth it," I grabbed her hand and pulled her up so we could go to my bedroom. She didn't hesitate, and I loved how comfortable she felt around me. For some reason, I didn't want to rush her once we got upstairs. Usually, I would be anxious for a girl to be naked, face down and ass up. Instead, I handed her a white tee from my drawer and found a towel and rag.

"You can shower first. The bathroom is through there." I pointed to the door next to the closet. Once I heard the water cut on, I went to shower in the hall bathroom. I washed up and brushed my teeth before throwing on some basketball shorts. "Damn," I said low as I walked back in the room and saw her standing there. She was by the door, her hands in front of her as she waited on me. "Yo why you ain't sit down on the bed or something," I asked as I moved closer.

"I didn't want to be rude," she said shrugging her shoulders, causing my shirt to slide down even more on her slender frame. She was tiny compared to me, and even though the shirt came down past her knees, it left her shoulders bare. Slowly I walked towards her and picked her up. I kissed her on her neck, and I felt her body stiffen. I could tell she wasn't used to being around a man.

"Relax ma, we ain't got to do shit you don't want to." Shit where did that thought come from. She was here for a reason. I set her on the bed and adjusted my dick before I got in with her. Bella grabbed my remote control like she was running my shit and flipped the TV on. I groaned when she turned it to Love and Hip Hop. "Hell naw shorty, anything but this. The news, some cooking show, romantic comedy. What else ya'll females be watching?" She gave me a fake pouty face before giggling and turning the channel to a comedy. I really didn't give a fuck what was on TV, I was too busy watching her. The way her whole face lit up when she smiled, how she had pulled her hair back into a ponytail but still looked sexy as fuck, had me intrigued.

"You ok?" she asked, her face really looked concerned.

"Nah," I said frowning.

"You want me to get you something?" Bella reached her hand out to gently touch my arm. I could barely focus after feeling how soft her skin was. I laughed low. She was asking could she get me some shit, but this was my crib.

"Come here," I said tugging her arms until she was sitting in front of me. I leaned her back, so she was resting on my chest. My hands wrapped around her body and I put my chin on top of her head. For the first time in a long time, my mind was able to relax. We stayed that way for a while, me enjoying the feel of her and her laughing at all the jokes on TV. My hand crept up her leg and then up under the t-shirt she had on. As soon as I found out she didn't have panties on, I felt myself get even harder. Yea I had to feel this pussy tonight.

I kissed her neck as my fingers found their way to her treasure. Lightly I ran my fingers over her clit causing her to jump some. Sticking one finger inside shorty pussy, her whole body locked up, and her eyes got wide. Moving her from in front of me I laid her on the bed and looked down at her. "Bella, we don't have to do this. I can take you home, or to a hotel or something. I mean I ain't about to force you to fuck, but if you stay here, that's kind of what's up." I wanted to give her options, she was acting like she was scared, and I knew I should have left her alone.

"I don't want to leave. I want this," she said even though her eyes told me something else. Shit maybe she was scared to go home. Her sister probably lived there and from the looks of it she was going to give her hell the next time she saw her.

"Listen, you can sleep in one of the guest rooms if you want." I couldn't believe I even had a girl in my crib, now I wasn't even going to get any. This shit was wild as fuck. I couldn't let my brother and cousin find out about this. They would be clowning me for sure.

"Sire, I knew what was up when I left with you. It's just my first time, so I don't really know what I should be doing. But believe me, I'm sure about this. Please don't make me leave." When she said it was her first time, I didn't even have words, why the fuck was she coming home with some random nigga from the club to lose her virginity. Sitting up, I put my head in my hands and groaned. What the fuck was I supposed to do now. I always knew my next move, so this was new.

"Ma, look I ain't the one to be breaking you in or none of that shit. You seem cool as fuck, but I just ain't the one." She slid off the bed, and I could see the sadness all over her face.

"It's cool, I understand," she said sniffling as she grabbed her clothes from the chair I had in the corner. "I can find my own way home," she stated as she took off my t-shirt and reached for her clothes. I felt my breath catch in my throat as she stood there naked. Bella's body was the fucking truth, her skin was smooth without even a scratch on her. I could barely focus, that's how she had me gone.

"Why me?" I asked as I got up and moved closer to her.

She stopped and turned to face me. "It was time, and when I met you, I thought you were special. I just couldn't see someone else taking my virginity. But my sister was right, you're not into inexperienced girls."

"Fuck," I muttered as I towered over her and pulled her into my arms. Before she could say anything, I leaned down and kissed her. Bella slightly parted her lips, and I slipped my tongue inside. I grabbed her soft ass and lifted her up causing her to wrap her legs around my waist. I kept telling myself I was her first, and to be honest instead of stressing me out, that shit had me feeling special. Walking her to the bed, I laid her down and stared at her wet pussy. Shorty's legs fell to the side of her body and gave me the perfect view. I was ready to beat up inside her walls, but I knew this shit wasn't going to be that easy.

Kissing up her legs she started to get stiff again. "Bella, relax, I ain't bout to hurt you." I felt her loosen up some as I spread her lower lips. I stroked her with my fingers gently before letting my tongue replace them. I lightly sucked on her clit causing her to grip my head. Easing one finger into her tight hole, I slowly fucked her while eating her pussy. She was moaning and trying to crawl backwards on the bed. I used my free arm to hold her in place as I continued to gently tease her. Finally, she cried out my name as she came. I licked up every drop, and I swear her juices tasted so sweet. I didn't stop licking and sucking on her until I felt her ready to cum again.

✣ 3 ✣

ARABELLA

HE HAD me feeling shit I ain't never felt before, it was like my body was on fire. I literally felt like I was going to explode, and then I did, and he was there slurping up my juices as my hand made its way to the curls on his head. Slowly he worked his way up my body, and I could feel his big ass dick poking against the inside of my thigh. As soon as the head touched my slit, I damn near jumped up off the bed. He whispered in my ear, "ma this shit is going to hurt no matter what I do. But I swear that pain won't last." I wasn't stupid, I knew this wasn't going to be the best I ever had. I've been hearing horror stories about a girls first time since as long as I could remember.

I waited, my body so still I wasn't even sure if I was breathing. Instead of just forcing his way inside of me, he slowly kissed me. I never thought I would be ok with tasting myself, but if anything, it turned me on. He ran his big hands up and down my back, and I felt my body shiver. His lips moved to my neck, and I felt his teeth sink into my flesh. "Sire," I moaned out his name and clawed his back. I knew I wanted something, but I had no idea what it was. Suddenly he rolled onto his back, taking me with him.

I wanted to reach out and touch the tattoos on his cut-up

chest. He was so sexy to me, and I wished my life was different. That I had a chance to make him my boyfriend, even though he definitely didn't seem like the settling down type. I didn't know where to set my hands, my ass was nervous and didn't want to just be touching him anywhere. "You good ma," he said as he took my hand and placed it on his chest. "You ain't never got to be afraid to touch me." I traced the tattoo he had of a crown on a lion's head. My hand wandered to the space above his heart and lingered there. I could feel his heartbeat strong underneath my touch.

Everything about him was turning me on, but at the same time making me feel a connection, one I had never felt before. As if my body had a mind of its own, I started grinding against his hard dick. He grabbed my ass, caressing me with his big hands, and I had that feeling of wanting to explode again. I came so hard I was shaking, I heard myself whimpering like a hurt animal. I could feel how wet I was, and it was embarrassing knowing I was dripping all over him. Resting my head on his chest, I couldn't even look his way. "Hold your head up, that's what a real nigga is supposed to do, make you feel good." He forced me to look at him and kissed my lips again. I felt him positioning me so that he was at my entrance. It felt ok at first until he started stretching me and then suddenly stopped.

"You can take control, take your own time," he said letting me slowly work him in and out of me. It was like every time it started to feel good, he slipped in a little deeper, and that shit was fucking me up. I was frustrated I couldn't just fit all of him inside of me and be done. Whenever I took him all the way out to give myself a break, he made a face like I was killing him.

"Sire, can you just get it over with please. I'm scared," I admitted closing my eyes.

He didn't say anything just held me close, suddenly he pushed himself all the way inside me, and I felt something tear. "Damn girl, this shit is tight as fuck," he said in my ear as he slowly moved my body, so I was riding him. As much as this shit hurt, it felt amazing just being this close to him. Feeling him inside of my body caused me to shiver. When he took my nipple into his mouth and gently sucked, I almost melted. I began moving my body slowly as he sat back and watched. He was so sexy to me, the way his eyes got darker as they roamed my body and how he bit his bottom lip. Everything about Sire made me want him.

"That's it girl, take your dick," he coached. And I felt the pain slightly start to go away now that I was in control. After a little while, I knew I was going to cum, my legs locked around his sides, and I scraped my nails over his chest. "That's it Bella, come for me baby."

"Sire," I cried out, confused that something that just hurt like hell now had me ready to never stop. I was so close to feeling something great that I started to pop my pussy faster and sink myself deeper on to him chasing that feeling. I felt myself shudder as he palmed my ass and went deeper. Then I felt him throbbing before he nut inside of me.

I couldn't move so I just laid there wondering was this nigga going to kick me out. I knew I should get up. I came to get fucked, and that was why he took me home and now the deed was done. I tried to push myself up since I was sinking into the plush King size bed. "The fuck you going," he said. Not giving me a chance to respond Sire wrapped his arms around me tight as hell. Not wanting to struggle, I relaxed against his bare chest. I fell asleep to the beating of his heart and a feeling of being safe, something I hadn't felt in a long time.

❧

I WOKE UP SUDDENLY. My belly was cramping, and I had to pee bad as hell. I tried to get up and felt something pinning me to the bed. I started to panic before I remembered where I was and who I was with. I was scared to move, but my bladder was about to burst, so I shoved at Sire's muscular arm and finally was able to scoot off the bed. After just one time, this nigga had me walking funny. I grabbed the towel I used the night before as I hobbled into the bathroom. Once I peed, I noticed the blood when I wiped and felt the shock of what I did wash over me. I didn't think I would be a virgin forever, but as much as I liked Sire, I felt like I was forced into this shit. Not by him, but by my circumstances. He didn't do shit wrong, he treated me like I was his girl and it was my first time. Instead of a hoe he brought in from the club, which in reality is what I had become. I turned on the shower, stepping in I felt the tears mix in with the hot water.

I stayed in the shower until the water ran cold. It actually felt good against my now sensitive pussy. I knew my bestie wouldn't believe any of this shit I did tonight and the thought of her reaction made me giggle a little. By the time I got out, dried off and put on some of his Vaseline lotion, the sun was fully up in the sky. I crept in the bedroom, hoping to put my clothes on and bounce before he woke up. I was praying the whole time that an Uber from way out here wasn't going to break me. He lived in the extreme suburbs.

I was wiggling into my jeans when I felt someone near me. "Yo, the fuck you think you going?" he asked standing over me. For a second, all I could think about was the way he was fucking me last night and the way everything he said sounded aggressive. I guess I loved that bad boy shit. I wanted him to pull me into his arms and kiss my neck than even lower. My mind wanted me to get naked and crawl back into his bed, but my pussy was asking was a bitch crazy.

Deciding to face him, I spun around and looked him in the eyes. They seemed lighter in the brightness from the sun, almost gold instead of honey-colored. "I was going home. I mean you got what you wanted." His face turned dark when I said that. "I mean what we both wanted to happen," I stuttered backtracking to try and keep him calm. He looked like he was hard to handle when he was angry. "Thank you Sire, I really mean that. You made my first time special. It was a night I will never forget." He grabbed me before I could walk away to find my corset. I wished I had a t-shirt that I could just slip on. I looked down and noticed he had my phone in his hand. For some reason, I felt my heart drop.

"Why you ain't tell me it was your birthday ma." I shrugged and looked down. It wasn't something worth celebrating, but I didn't want to tell him that. "You looking all sad and shit, what's wrong?"

"Nothing, it's just another day." *Just a day that I will be raped and abused*, I thought to myself. He stood there, flipping my phone over and over in his palm, looking like he was in deep thought. Suddenly he moved even more into my space causing me to back up. It didn't help, he followed me until my back was against the wall, and my breath was caught in my throat.

"Who the fuck is Alex," he asked and my hands got clammy as I fought with myself not to break down and tell him my situation. "Tell that nigga to stop fucking texting you. You busy for the day." He looked hella serious, and I felt a small smile form on my lips.

He handed me my phone, and I saw all the texts from friends and family wishing me a Happy Birthday. Alex had sent me a message that simply said- *Can't wait to see you later.* That made me shudder, and I damn near threw the iPhone in the trash. I knew I had to go home, but it was the last fucking place I wanted to be. Sighing I finished buttoning my jeans after removing Sire's hands from my body. "I have to go," I said, my voice laced with regret.

4

SIRE

"STAY WITH ME FOR THE WEEKEND," I said causing her to look at me with shock on her face. To be honest, I was shocked as fuck too. I never spent time with these hoes outside of busting em down and sending em home. There was just something about Arabella, I didn't want her out of my presence. I sure as fuck didn't want her leaving to go see bitch ass Alex. I didn't want to share her with anyone. I felt like she belonged to me.

Shorty stared at me, her head to the side like she was thinking about something. "Ok, I guess that would be cool. I don't have any clothes or anything so we gonna have to stay in." She was so timid. Any other girl would have had one hand in my pocket and on my money so I could cop them some new shit. But not her, she was cool with spending her birthday weekend doing the Netflix and chill thing.

"Let me shower fast, and we can hit the mall and get you some shit to wear. It's your day, so after we eat and shop, we can do whatever you want. That sure as fuck ain't sitting in the house and watching TV." I smiled at her, and she gave me back a shy smile. "Yo, you pretty as fuck, keep that smile on your face." I slapped her on the ass as I made my way to shower. After handling my hygiene, I threw on some Balmain jeans and a hoodie along with some fresh wheat Timbs. I grabbed a stack from my safe and went to find baby girl. She was standing in the kitchen with a confused look on her face.

"Sire, I was trying to cook, but umm, there is nothing to cook." She was sipping on some water and giving the boxes of cereal I had a disgusted look. I laughed, I swear she was looking at those boxes like they fucked her nigga and she wanted to fight.

"Come on we can get breakfast first if you can't wait and you can grab some groceries and shit later." She nodded as we walked out of the door. I was used to bitches constantly talking like they had never heard of a silent moment, but Bella was just able to be present without chatting my ears off. I could tell she was uncomfortable in last night's clothes, so I hit Chick-Fila drive-thru and grabbed us some food. I felt bad as fuck she was eating a damn breakfast bowl on her birthday, but I was going to make it up to her later.

"So, tell me about yourself. I mean all I know is that you were a virgin and today is your birthday and shit. What's your favorite color, favorite food, all that good shit," I said as I sat my seat back further. She chewed a little while looking thoughtful.

"I just turned eighteen today, I'm graduating high school in the spring. I love to cook, my favorite color is blue, and I love seafood. I'm pretty laid back. I have fun doing whatever. I will pretty much try anything once." I smirked when she said that thinking about the things I would love for he to try just one time with me. "So what about you?"

"Shit what about me ma, you see a nigga, ain't much else to me." She put her trash in the empty bag we had sitting between us. I was mesmerized as I watched her wipe her juicy lips with a napkin. Little proper ass.

"There is more to you than just being a nigga in the streets. I know it." She finished up her little speech with a sexy ass wink.

"I'm *that* nigga in the streets," I replied winking back. Not being able to resist, I leaned over and kissed her before starting up the truck and driving towards the mall. I pulled up to the main door and double-parked. Handing shorty some bread she just stared at the money.

"You not coming in with me?" she asked, and I heard the sadness in her voice. Normally I wouldn't have been seen walking around a fucking mall with any female. But Arabella had me on some other shit.

"Naw ma, run in and cop one of those sparkly sweatsuits ya'll be wearing and some sneakers, then come back and change in here. Then we going to shut the fucking mall down together." She slowly took the money and gave me another one of her award-winning smiles. That shit had my dick hard as fuck. She wasn't even in the stores a good twenty minutes before she came back out with a pink striped bag and another one from Foot Locker. She must have changed in the bathroom because instead of the club clothes shorty was rocking a black sweatsuit and a pair of black and white air maxes on her feet. She had pulled her hair back into a ponytail, and even though she was casual she still looked good. The way she was smiling at a nigga had me feeling like a fucking king. I pulled into a parking spot and threw her bags inside.

"Here Sire, your change," Bella said handing me back most of the money I gave her.

I glared at her hand like she was handing me shit. "Shorty what kind of niggas you be fucking wit? Stop fucking disrespecting me," I growled. I didn't know why I was even mad about a bitch giving me my money back. I didn't know if Arabella was bad for me or what, because she sure had me breaking rules.

"Shit, I been around no niggas, rude ass," she said shrugging and pocketing the money. Her face had a slight frown like I had really offended her.

Hearing that she hadn't spent time with a bunch of other niggas had improved my mood. "Come on Bells don't do that," I said walking up behind her and kissing her on the neck. Shorty smelled good as fuck, and I know I ain't have no girly shit in my house, so it had to just be her. We hit up Nordstrom's, and she held back like I was in here for my benefit. I saw her eyes land on a bunch of shit though. "Ma, you don't want those boots?" I asked as she eyed some Uggs with bows all down the back. My sister loved those overpriced boots, and I had bought her at least five pairs this year.

She picked up the price tag and dropped it fast as hell like it burned her hands. "Nope, I'm good. Just along for the ride."

"Yo, this is your ride shorty. I don't be in the mall chilling and shit. What's your shoe size?" I shoved her a little causing her to push me back, it was cute seeing her try and move me since I at least had eighty pounds on her.

"Fine, size eight. You can buy me one pair and thank you."

Leaning down, I kissed her making sure to slide my tongue inside her mouth and pull her into my body. She moaned, and I wanted to snatch her clothes off in the store and get some more of her bomb pussy. "See how you got a nigga fucked up," I whispered, letting her go, but not before I made sure she felt how hard I was. Shorty blushed but had a smirk on her face. Catching the salesgirl's eye, I waved her over.

"Hello, how can I help you today?" She said while licking her lips and standing close to me. Her ass was hittin', even though I could tell some corner boy spent all his bread financing it. Normally, I would have had her on her knees later that night, but being around Bella it was easy to only focus on her.

I made sure to step back some and grill her. "First of all, stop licking those crusty ass lips, I ain't interested." Bella snorted, but lightly elbowed me in the ribs at the same time.

"Sire, be nice," she hissed while trying not to laugh.

"I am being nice. Hell, I never mentioned her shape, her ass is fat but the rest of her looks like a fucking banana. She stepped her sloped shape ass to me after seeing you and me in here together." People around me started laughing, and the salesgirl frowned up her face. "Now go get my girl a pair of those boots in every color size eight." I gave Arabella a look daring her to say shit. For the rest of the day, I dragged her from store to store buying everything her gaze landed on. I made sure she didn't touch the money I gave her before. For the first time, I spent coins on a female who wasn't related to me, and it wasn't that bad, now I knew why my brother was always tricking on his girl.

"Damn Sire I know you tired, and so am I. I don't even know where I'm going to put all this stuff. I don't even need so many things." She was starting to look sleepy for real, and the mall wasn't even all I had planned for the day.

"Aight, go grab my truck and meet me in the front sleeping beauty. You know how to drive, right? Don't fuck up my whip," I warned passing her the key fob. She rolled her eyes as she snatched the key and skipped off to the parking lot. I hurried and went to Kay's jewelry store we had just left out of not long ago. Shorty got some diamond earrings, but I saw how she looked at the charm bracelet. I remembered what she told me when we first walked in the mall, that the best gifts had meaning. And for some reason, I wanted to get her a gift that meant something to her.

❧

"SIRE," Bella cried out my name as I gave her long strokes. I never even meant to sex shorty, at least not right now, but when she stripped for her shower I couldn't walk away. I was just happy she was enjoying this dick. The way she was whimpering let me know she was about to cum and I was ready for it.

"It's ok baby let me feel you cum." I stopped to suck on her stiff nipples, I swear God gave shorty a body close to perfection. She even had a small beauty mark on her breasts. As soon as I felt her body arch and she got even wetter I knew she was close. Grabbing her ass, I brought her closer and trapped her screams in my mouth. I nutted deep in her womb, not even thinking about not having a condom on. A part of me felt free to not strap up with her since I was the first to ever get the pussy. "Come on, we got to go shorty," I slapped her on her sweaty skin as I got up.

"Nooo, we been gone all day. I thought it was my day. Maybe we could just do that again," she said smirking at my semi-hard dick. As tempting as it was, I had some shit planned, so I hit the shower leaving her to sulk. I got out and put on a button-up Armani shirt and a pair of Armani jeans. I wasn't into no suit and tie shit, but I wanted to look nice.

"Here, wear the black dress you got," I said placing it on the bed. "We bout to go have dinner." Her face lit up as she went into the bathroom to get ready. Baby girl came out looking like new fucking money. She had her hair down her back, and the dress was hugging all her curves. I couldn't believe she was only eighteen, she looked like she was a grown ass woman.

I led her to the truck, trying not to let her sexy ass distract me. I drove to Black and Blue and parked. Pulling up to Valet, I allowed him to help her out of the truck while I grabbed the gift bag I had from the back. Grabbing Bella's hand, we walked inside. I was happy my little sister was able to help me out at the last minute, the table had roses, balloons and the custom cake I had her grab and bring to the restaurant for me. I led her to the table in the corner and held out her chair so she could sit down. "Oh my God Sire, you did all of this for me? Thank you so much!" She was grinning and jumping up and down in her chair like a little kid.

"You good ma, just wanted to make sure your day was special." We ordered, and she snapped some pictures of the set up, I was sure to post on some social media shit. After we ate, I handed her the gift bag. She took the box out slowly, her face already bawled up with tears falling. She opened the box and gingerly removed the charm bracelet. I only had them put four charms on there, a heart, a star, a chef's hat and the letter A. I figured I could buy her some other ones for her next birthday or some shit. I had no idea what me and shorty was going to have after this weekend. But I just knew I didn't want to let her out of my life. Maybe it was that new pussy that had me cashing out on her ass and playing mister romantic. Or maybe it was just her, she was't like any of the hoes I normally fucked with.

"Thank you Sire, thank you so much. This was the perfect gift, the perfect day. I couldn't have imagined this in my dreams." She held her hand out so I could put her bracelet on her, but she was still crying and shit.

"Come here," I said pulling her up so she could come sit in my lap. She curled her body into mine and rested her head on my chest. "You deserve this shit ma and more. I'm going to always make your days the best I can. Now stop crying these white folks looking at me like I done hit ya ass or something." She laughed and looked up at me, even with her watery eyes she was the baddes girl I had ever seen. I had no idea how, but shorty had my heart in just one day.

5

RUMOR

I HEARD the phone buzz again, and I sighed in annoyance. My baby kicked the shit out of me, almost like he knew it wasn't time for us to get up yet. I double-checked, my eyes peering around the curtains to the outside, and yep it was still pitch black. It was definitely still the middle of the fucking night. Back to back, the text messages came in, but this nigga remained asleep. Reaching next to him, I grabbed both phones to see messages on both screens. Not one of them was business-related unless Jackie asking to buy his dick counted. I rolled my eyes hard as fuck, but that just pissed me off more because it wasn't like he could see me.

This was the shit I didn't need, definitely not right now, I had too much other stuff going on. Using my foot, I kicked the shit out of his side. "The fuck you doing Rumor, damn, a nigga trying to sleep." He rolled over, his light brown eyes narrowed as he grilled me. The look he was giving me would have put fear into anyone, but not me. Remee was never aggressive with me, he was all bark and no bite.

I threw the phones at him, causing one to catch him on the chin. I laughed when he winced in pain, then tried to act tough like that shit didn't hurt. "Come on, ma, what's wrong?" He tried to pull me close to him, and any other time I would have given in. I loved being in Remee's arms, my head on his bare chest, listening to his heartbeat. But the me who was tired of having her feelings hurt was over it.

"Remee, just go the fuck home. I'm sick of this shit. Just like you trying to sleep, so are your son and me. But we can't because every bitch in the town is texting you, hoping you will throw some dick their way. Like for real, why do you even have two fucking phones if these hoes call on both of them?" I rolled over and hid my face in the pillow. I was too young for this shit, I had loved Remee since the first day I saw him when I was only twelve years old. But I just wasn't sure if love was enough anymore.

The room lit up as he unlocked one of his phones, and the buzzing abruptly stopped. "Yo Jackie, why the fuck you keep calling me and shit. Your stupid ass disturbing my baby mom's sleep. Don't hit my fucking line again." I heard Jackie on the other end, calling me all types of bitches and shit, but I was used to that. Every time he cheated on me with them, or them with me, since I was basically the fool, these girls called me every name in the book. I had fought so many females I could have been a professional fucking boxer at this point. "Come on Rumor, I handled that shit."

"Remee, I meant what I said. Just leave and don't come back. On some real shit, I don't even know why I agreed to have this baby wit you. I have nothing, no real money, no family that gives a fuck about me, no man. I played myself." I could see his face get dark and I knew I pushed him, but for the first time ever I really didn't give a fuck. For once, my feelings of hurt were stronger than me worrying about anything else. I jumped up to get the fuck out of the room so he could leave, but I didn't pay attention and tripped over his Timbs that were next to the bed. Falling damn near flat on my face. I used my hands to catch myself just in time, so I didn't hurt my baby.

"The fuck is wrong with you Rumor, my baby better fucking

be ok," he snapped loud as hell as he tried to pick me up. I cut my eyes at him as I got up using the bed as support.

"First of all, lower your damn voice, you know my mom doesn't know about the baby," I hissed hoping no one was awake to hear this fight. If my mom found out I was pregnant, my son and I would be living in someone's homeless shelter. She was serious as a fucking heart attack about not taking care of no babies or even allowing them in her house. Shit, it's not like she took care of my sister and me anyway. But either way, she had made her position on the situation clear. "Second of all move your fucking shoes, that's what caused me to fall. My son is straight, but it's time for you to go. I don't even want to see your face right now."

"Rumor, I'm sick of this shit. You need to tell your mom about our son, asap. I don't give a fuck if she hears me or not. I ain't no damn kid, and you act like I can't take care of ya'll! You are riding in a brand-new fucking BMW, no note or nothing. Anything you want I get you. I have been telling you to let me move you up out of here. You don't need nobody for shit, so don't act like you do." He came to stand in between my legs and forced me to look up at him. I hated that my hormones had me craving his touch. "Why you have to be so hardheaded Ru, what else a nigga gotta do?"

"I can't depend on you A'Remee, yo dick is for every fucking body. So nothing with you is stable. You want to move me into some ducked off place, not where you lay your head. You will never slow down. What happens when you start taking care of your newest bitch, and its fuck me and our son? I can't go out like that. I have to figure this shit out for myself because I'm all I got." Saying it out loud caused the tears to come once again. I literally felt crushed, just knowing I was alone in this world had me depressed as fuck.

"You don't get it. Yea my dick was friendly as fuck. A nigga was young and dumb, but I been cleaning that shit up. We bout to have a baby, you the only girl I give a fuck about. These birds can't even get a damn Happy Meal. When I'm in these streets risking it all, it ain't for me, it's for you two." His hand rubbed my small baby bump, and I felt so conflicted. Could I trust Remee to be there when I needed him?

He lifted me up and sat on the bed with me in his lap. As soon as he started kissing my tears away, I knew what was coming next. His lips made their way to my neck and softly started sucking. And my body betrayed me just like that. I felt his dick get harder beneath me, and my juices immediately started to drip. I kept trying to talk to my pussy and tell her to chill, but that hoe was already grinding all over him. Her mind was set on only one thing, feeling him deep inside of me. By the time he started kissing my lips, I had his dick out and at my opening. Slowly I lowered myself onto him, inch by inch he still stretched me after all these years. Remee took my virginity when I was just fifteen years old, and he was the only boy I had even kissed.

"See how hard I get for you. This dick belongs to you Rumor, a nigga only loves you." He was saying all the right things, and while he was making love to me, everything else faded away. I came back to back, and I was ready to fall out, this baby had me weak as fuck. Remee grabbed my ass, and I felt him go even deeper. At this point, he was doing all the work, and all I could do was moan. As much as this felt wrong, this shit felt good. He always knew my spots, like he was made just to sex me. I felt him throbbing, and I knew he was about to bust. I let my nails sink into his back as my body caught up, and we came together. As soon as the blood stopped rushing to my head, all I heard was his phones still going off. We were right back to the place we started from. His arms tightened around me like he was afraid I was going to run away.

"Remee, just go. Be free, I don't want to be with someone who has to try so hard not to fuck other girls. You deserve your freedom and happiness, and random pussy is what makes you happy. Your son will be around when you want to see him. You don't have to worry about us." I wiggled out of his grip and climbed off his lap. Getting back onto the bed, I held my pillow for comfort as Remee got up. He stood there watching me for a while. I was sure he didn't expect this, never thought I would turn him away. I was supposed to be the good side chick. The one he kept at home, for when he got bored. And for so long I had been, my love for him winning out over my self-respect. And now I just didn't know what to do.

I held my breath when he moved and watched out of the corner of my eye as he put his clothes and shoes on, then his jewelry and last he grabbed his gun. He turned to look at me and started to say something, his eyes filled with sadness. Instead of speaking, he threw some money on the dresser and left.

LEAVING THE DOCTOR'S OFFICE, I sat in my car and felt the hot tears as they dripped onto my lap. I had been calling and texting Remee since he left my house two weeks ago and he hasn't responded. And now he missed my doctor's appointment. I really could have used him today because the doctor wasn't happy with my blood pressure and wanted me on bed rest. It wasn't like Rem to miss the baby's appointments; he never has since we found out I was pregnant no matter what he had going on in the streets. I had never gone this long without talking to him since we met, and it was fucking me up. I looked at the unread text messages and wondered was he ok. I had been going back and forth between thinking he was hurt or locked up, or thinking he was just ignoring me to be with another bitch. I went to my contacts, and my finger hovered over his mothers' number. Shaking my head, I threw the phone in my Louis Vuitton bag and sighed. Even though I had a good relationship with Remee's family, I didn't want to be that girl, calling them every time we had a problem.

Driving I couldn't get Remee off my mind, even though I was

disappointed in him, I still loved him. Nothing we went through had ever changed the way I felt about him. Maybe he was tired of me, maybe I had pushed him too far this time. I knew I needed to tell my mom about our son, I had to put on my big girl panties and get the shit over with. I was just trying to save a little more money, so if shit went left, naw when shit went left, I could be ready to move right away. So far, I had five thousand dollars saved up. I only wanted two thousand more so I could pay up a few months of rent since I wouldn't be able to work when the baby came.

Making a u-turn, I knew I had to go and talk to Remee. The whole drive to his house, I thought about what I was going to say. I had never really apologized to Rem before. I mean partly because he was always doing wrong, thinking with his dick. And partly because he had me spoiled as fuck, so I never really felt like I was wrong even when I was. Pulling up, I parked behind his black Range Rover and stepped out. I wished I had gone home and changed first, I felt bummy in my tights and plain t-shirt. But I knew once I went into the house, I wasn't coming back out. Using my key, I let myself in. My stomach was in knots for some reason. What if Remee rejected me, told me he didn't give a fuck about the baby or me? As much as I told him he might do that shit, I never actually believed it deep down inside.

I didn't see him downstairs, but I smelled weed smoke and noticed a bunch of empty bottles of Henny on the table. He must have been going through something to be drinking all that liquor. I felt a tinge of guilt, wondering if it was because of me. "Remee," I called as I walked up the stairs. By the time I waddled to the top, he was coming out of his bedroom at the end of the hall. He stood there with only a wife beater and some Ethika boxers on. My eyes roamed his body, and I felt my pussy jump. Remee would always be the sexiest man to me. His coco brown skin and golden colored eyes were everything.

"Rumor, the fuck you doing here?" he asked, sounding annoyed and I felt my face fall.

"I came to apologize, you never came to the appointment, so I was worried." I could see guilt in his eyes when I mentioned the appointment. "The doctor wanted me on bed rest–" Before I could finish my sentence, he was in front of me and had his hand on my belly.

"Damn ma, I fucked up. Ya'll alright? A nigga broke his phone and ain't replaced that shit yet. I should have been checking on you. I just been in a bad headspace. Man fuck," he yelled as he punched a hole in the wall next to me. I had never seen Remee this mad over something so sall, and I had to wonder for what. If anything, I was the one who should have been mad.

"I mean I hear you on breaking your phone, but I called and texted both of your lines and nothing. I know you not really feeling me, but I thought you would have at least gave a fuck about our son." I couldn't read the look on his face, and I almost wished I wouldn't have come at him so hard. But fuck that, his excuse sounded lame, and I couldn't just let the shit go.

"Rumor, give me a fucking break ma. If I would have seen your calls, I would have hit you back. As long as ya'll are good, that shit don't matter." He took me in his arms and rested his head in my neck. "I'm not trying to keep arguing with you. I love you too much for that, just leave shit alone sometimes." The minute I felt his arms around me, I started to relax, I needed this man like I needed air. I guess once again I was about to be a fool for love.

"Remee, when are you coming back to bed," a female's voice called from behind me causing me to jerk myself out of his arms. Standing at his bedroom doorway was a butt-naked female. But not just any female, it was my sisters' best friend.

"Fuck," Remee said as he ran his hand over his dreads. I had to hold on to the wall to keep from falling out. I felt dizzy and sick all at the same time, and I was damn near crumpled onto the floor. To think I was coming here to apologize, and he had this shit going on. No wonder he hadn't gotten his phone fixed or saw any of the calls and texts I sent to his business line. He was too busy fucking this bitch.

"Rumor, I don't know why you over there looking all shocked and shit. This been going on for months and that nigga dick is for everybody anyway. He has never given a fuck about you, you're not even his girl. So, pick up your face boo and leave with some dignity." Jillian stood there with a smirk on her face, not even attempting to hide her body.

"Come here, Rumor," he snapped, but I didn't move. Fuck Remee right now.

"Rem, it's all good, I'm gonna go on and get out of your way," I said as I stood up fully, giving myself a pep talk to get it the fuck together. My hand automatically went to my belly because it felt like my son was punching and kicking me at the same damn time. I knew he was stressed the fuck out because I was.

Before I could move good this hoe was racing towards me. "Remee, is this bitch pregnant? After you forced me to kill our baby, you allowed her to keep one?" My eyes bucked, he was really over here having a whole situationship with my sisters' best friend. Raw sex and all. This hoe had to be lying, but the look on his face told me she wasn't, and I felt a pain like I had never felt before.

"Bitch shut the fuck up, don't say shit to her. Get dressed and bounce," Remee snapped, gripping her arm hard as fuck before she got to me. Except it didn't even matter. I was over him, this was the final straw, no way I could ever trust him now. This was crossing a line. All I could hear was Jillian's words telling me I wasn't even his girl, then asking why she couldn't keep her baby. She was right about one thing, I wasn't shit to him. I guess I should have gotten an abortion too.

I backed down the hall as fast as I could. I had to get out of here. Remee tried to reach out for me, but I ran down the stairs and outside. I made sure to throw his house key back inside before slamming the door and going to my car. If I didn't need a way home, I would have left this mother fucker right here too. I didn't want anything that Remee bought me, gave me or did for me in my life anymore. He would never change, never grow the fuck up. How could pussy be that important to him? I always thought having his baby meant something, but I guess that I was just one of many. How could he let this shit happen? Didn't he understand this would break me, or did he even care?

I sped home, barely able to see through my tears. My phone was blowing up, everyone from Remee to his momma, sister and even his brother were calling me. But I wasn't in any place to speak to any fucking body. Seeing my sister's Malibu parked in the driveway, I pulled in and hopped out as fast as my pregnant body would allow. I flung open the front door so hard I hurt my hand. "What's your problem?" my sister said, her head popped up from her phone as she rolled her eyes at me, then smirked. That told me her bestie already told her about the situation.

"Yea you know what's wrong with me you dirty bitch," I said as I grabbed her by the lace front, she had on. "How could you let your slack-ass friend fuck my man and not say shit? Why would you even allow this shit to happen," I shouted as I started giving her nothing but head shots. My sister wasn't a punk, but my adrenaline was taking over because she couldn't even get a word in, let alone a hit.

Seeing the blood squirt from her nose only caused me to go harder. I wanted to knock her fucking head off. Feeling a hard-ass kick from my baby that caused pain to go down my spine, I stepped back, letting her body crumple to the carpet in front of the couch. "Bitch, you broke my nose," she screamed as the door opened, and my mother walked in. Her pretty hazel eyes got wide, and her hand came to her chest like she was about to have a heart attack. But I knew better, she didn't have a weak bone in her body. And a fight wasn't about to make her lose control.

"What the hell is going on in my house," she damn near growled. Her eyes turned into mean slits as she glared at both my sister and me. One thing with May Ann Fisher, she didn't give a fuck about her kids equally. Her dick appointments, Peach

Cîroc and bundles, came before us along with many other things, like her furniture. "You better not get blood on my damn couch. I don't care if you both kill each other. I just better not see any damage to any of my shit." She turned to leave but stopped in her tracks when my sister began to speak as she slowly rose from the floor.

"Rumor, as soon as I get my hands on you, I'm fucking you up, and I don't give a damn about that baby your carrying."

"Come again, little girl? Who is carrying a fucking baby and thinks they are going to live in my house?" My mother was like one of those police dogs who was about to sniff out the truth. She moved closer to me and squinted her eyes. Having seen whatever she needed, she nodded her head in confirmation. "Laquita don't even fucking touch her, I need her ass to be able to walk out of this house with all her shit because I ain't helping lift a damn thing." After warning my sister, she turned her gaze back to me, a look of disgust on her face. "You have an hour to pack your stuff and get out. I would say I'm surprised, but I'm not. I hope you realize that this little boy will not be there for you." She stood aside and waved her hand towards the stairs.

I simply nodded my head and went upstairs to get my things. It only took me thirty minutes to pack all my stuff in four suitcases and three duffel bags. I couldn't take the bed, TV or dressers, so it was mostly clothes, shoes and personal items. I had a few outfits I had picked up for my son, so I grabbed those as well. I made sure to carry everything to my car myself. I didn't want any help from anyone in this house of evil. My sister watched silently as I grabbed the last bag and headed for the door. "Key," was all my mother said as she stood in the front like the gatekeeper. I gently placed it in the palm of her hand and headed to my car. I had no idea where I was going for tonight, but I knew I would make it work.

THE CRAMP in my neck woke me up. I had spent the past few nights sleeping in my car. I didn't want to waste money on a hotel, and the place I applied for through housing authority wasn't ready yet. They told me Monday I could move in since they had some last-minute stuff to take care of. I mean it was the projects, so I wasn't sure what they had to prepare, but honestly, I was just grateful they bumped me up the list and got me a place. If I wasn't pregnant, I would have had to wait for months. The social worker who helped me said I could come in and stay at a homeless shelter, but I had heard horror stories about those places. I checked the clock on my car and knew I had to wake up and take my ass to school. I had been taking a shower in the gym before class, and the process was tiring. I was pretty sure this wasn't what the doctor considered bed rest. I prayed so much for the safety of my son; I was sure God was sick of hearing from me at this point.

Hearing a knock on the window, I damn near jumped out of my skin. Turning to look and see who the fuck it was, I frowned back at Remee's dark face. He had called me so much, and from so many different numbers, I had just turned my phone off. I didn't have any fucking body anyway, so I really didn't need it for anything. "Rumor, open the fucking door," he growled. Shaking my head, I hit the push to start but never got to hit the gas before he punched a hole through the glass and turned the car off. Before I could react, he had opened my door and drug me out of the car. His hand was cut and bleeding, but it didn't seem to slow him down. I stood up and brushed the glass off of me, I crossed my arms and slit my eyes.

"Remee look what the fuck you did to my window," I damn near screamed. I was so fucking frustrated because I couldn't sleep in a car missing a window. This was NY, even in the spring it got cold at night. My hand itched to slap the shit out of him, but that wasn't going to solve the problem. I prayed the insurance could have it fixed today, but this wasn't a hooptie. Everything with BMW was expensive and ran slow as fuck.

"I will make sure it's fixed, but you already knew that shit." He said like he wasn't standing there with a bloody hand. "I know you not sleeping in your fucking car? Especially while you carrying my seed." He was angry, I knew Remee well, and the way his golden eyes suddenly had green flecks told me all I needed to know. That shit had me backing up a few steps. "What you fucking scared of me now," he barked, before laughing like he had lost his mind. I felt a shiver down my spine and in this moment, I was scared of him, he was acting crazy as fuck.

"Remee don't act all fucking upset about me doing anything while carrying your son. Had I known I was just one of many baby momma's I would have did you the favor of having an abortion. I need to get to school and now try to fix my window are we done here?" Scared or not I didn't have time to just stand here all fucking day waiting on him to do whatever. He paced in front of me, every few minutes he would look up and glare my way, while his fists clenched and unclenched. I was pretty sure if I wasn't carrying his son, he would have already fucked me up.

"Yea it's like that Rumor, after all we been through you would kill our baby." He stopped in front of me and tugged my arms so that they fell at my sides. I was confused, I didn't really know how to respond or how to feel. Of course, I didn't want to kill our son, a baby that was created out of love. But I also didn't want to force no nigga into being a father if he wasn't interested. "Answer me, you hate a nigga that much?" I was crying as he wrapped me in his arms. He owed me an outfit now too because he was bleeding on my shirt. "Ru, I'm sorry, none of that shit was supposed to happen. I'm dumb as fuck for messing with Jillian, with any other girl. I don't expect you to give me another chance but let me get you and my son somewhere safe. I'm fucking begging you, at least let me do that."

"Why, Remee? Why am I never enough for you?" Just asking the question broke my heart. It felt like my insides were on fire as I held my breath waiting on him to respond.

"Ma, you more than enough. Don't ever forget that. Me fucking up isn't a reflection on you. That shit is all on me. I just can't get this relationship shit right, but you Rumor, are perfect. The kind of woman any man would dream of." He used his thumbs to wipe my tears away before leading me to his truck. I got inside feeling numb and watched as he wrapped his hand in a towel than grabbed all of my stuff and moved it to the back of his Range. Remee shook his head before pulling out his phone to call someone. Twenty minutes later, a tow truck showed up, and he spoke to the guy before getting in and driving away. At this point, I was going to be late for school, and I really didn't give a fuck, my day started off bad and seemed like it was on a downhill spiral.

I wanted to ask where he was taking me but had no energy left to fight. I just hoped for his sake it wasn't his house. I would never step foot in there again knowing he had been laid up with Jillian and God knows who else. I felt my nerves calm down some when he pulled up to his mother's house. Miss Layla was the sweetest person I had ever met, I wished daily that I had a mother like her. Unfortunately, the one I was *blessed* with was a prime example of continuing the cycle of hood rat shit.

As soon as we walked through the door, my stomach made a loud noise at the smell of pancakes. "I see you finally found her," Amira said as she walked over to Remee and snatched my duffel bag. Remee's sister was the closest thing to a best friend I had. Most females hated me because I had naturally long hair, flawless skin and a bad ass body. Or maybe it was because I was fucking Remee. Probably the last one. "Come and take a shower and you can tell me why you haven't answered your phone in days." She grilled Rem as she said the last part causing me to give a small smile.

I hurried to follow her upstairs before she punched her brother in his face. Amira was wild as fuck, mostly because her brothers and cousin spoiled her so she felt like she could get away with anything. As soon as the bedroom door closed, she was standing there with her hands on her hips and a raised eyebrow. Amira was also a drama queen. "Girl it's a long story, one that ended with me not fucking with Remee anymore, getting kicked out of my house and beating the piss out of my sister. Mira, I really don't want to talk about it." She nodded and came over to hug me. We stood that way for a minute before I took out my clothes and personal items so I could go shower. I eyed her king-sized bed and wished I could crawl in it and sleep for a good ten hours. Sighing, I went to handle my hygiene so I could get out of here.

I felt better once I was fresh, I threw on a pair of black stretchy tights and a pink scoop neck shirt that said Boujee on the front in black letters. I slid my swollen feet into some black flip flops and pulled my hair back into a messy bun. I wasn't even into my third trimester, and I felt like a beached whale. I wasn't going to complain though because my son was worth it. Making my way downstairs, I noticed Amira and her mom at the table along with my breakfast. "Good morning Miss Layla," I said as I slid onto the chair and grabbed my fork. I was starving, I had been living on McDonald's and chips the past few days.

"Good morning baby, go ahead and eat your food. And Rumor, if you ever do something so stupid again, I will personally go upside your head." I nodded, looking down at my plate in embarrassment. I didn't want the world to know I was sleeping in my car, but I guess Remee didn't give a fuck.

"I was just doing what I had to, but no need to worry I will be in my own apartment on Monday." She seemed satisfied with my answer because a smile graced her beautiful face. I didn't mention I would be in my car again tonight provided my window would be fixed. I would just keep that to myself.

"You ready," Remee said interrupting my thoughts. He stood there looking me over, trying to figure out if I was ok.

"Yes, thank you for breakfast Miss Layla and for letting me use your shower. I have to get to school now. Amira I will call you today before I go to work."

After saying my good-byes, I followed Remee outside so he could drop me off. He played music the whole ride, and I was happy we didn't have to force any small talk. I didn't have shit to say to his ass. Once we pulled up to Wilson High School, I hurried and grabbed my bookbag. "I would appreciate it if you have my car here at the end of the school day, fixed. I need to sleep in it tonight, and I need to get to work."

Remee grabbed me roughly before I could get out. Snatching my face around, his fingers gripped the shit out of my jaw. I damn near cried out it hurt so bad, but I didn't. I refused to give him the satisfaction. "Rumor, I swear ma, I'm trying to be patient, but you are about to get fucked up. Look at me," he barked, causing my eyes to fly to his face. "You not sleeping in a fucking car, not with my son, not if you weren't pregnant. Even if we are never together again, I'm always going to be yo nigga, I'm always taking care of you. I will pick you up after school, and Rumor, do not make me come and find you again." I felt a chill the way he said that shit. I rushed to get away from him and into the school, I wasn't beat for this shit today.

Every class seemed to go by fast as hell since I had to deal with Remee at the end of the day. Any other time they would have moved slow, and I would have been annoyed. The final bell rang, and I slowly made my way to my locker. I was leaving my bookbag here for the night since I had no homework. My back hurt from carrying all those fucking heavy books and shit. By the time I made it outside the buses had left and only a few kids were around. I didn't see Remee out front, so he was either late or parked in the lot. Huffing I made my way to the back of the school so I could go to the parking lot. "Yo Rumor," someone said, calling my name. Like I said I didn't have a lot of friends so I couldn't place her voice. Turning around, I came face to face with a metal pipe. Turning to run, I was hit by another pipe, only this time it connected with my hip and not my head. My heart was racing, and all I could think about was my baby.

I was surrounded by females who continued hitting me,

showing no mercy and no sign of letting up. I couldn't tell how many were there, but I knew I was outnumbered. Dropping to the ground, I did the only thing I could think of, curled into a ball and tried to protect my son. "Bitch, you didn't think I would let you keep this baby, did you? No, your baby is going to die just like mine did." That voice I recognized. Jillian was here to get her revenge. I was sobbing as I felt pain tear through my abdomen and back. I knew they had killed my son, I felt his life slipping away, just like mine. I tried to hold on to consciousness but realizing I had lost my baby. I didn't even care anymore.

✿ 6 ✿

REMEE

I PACED the hallway outside of Rumor's door praying, I didn't even know what I was praying for, but I knew I needed God at this point. I couldn't even think about the fact my son was dead or I would be on a murder spree. That was still happening, but not until I made sure Rumor was good. The love I had for her made it impossible to walk away. We had a special bond, always had and I took it for granted. I caused this shit, my carelessness. When I first got with Rumor I wasn't on bullshit, I never even looked at another girl. That was back when we both lived in the ghetto before I had a dime to my name. When I met her, she was just the quiet nerdy girl from next door. She was pretty as fuck if you ever got to see her face outside of a book.

The most amazing thing about Rumor was that she broke through Cahir's cold exterior. My cousin was damaged beyond repair, shit he still was, but Rumor treated him like he was a normal everyday nigga. She never gossiped about him or acted scared of him and for that she had his loyalty forever. That was how it all started, Cahir and I were playing football, and he threw the ball in her yard, knocking the book out of her hands. She jumped up from the steps and ran up on my cousin. I will never forget the way she jumped in his face, biting her bottom lip the whole time showing she was nervous, but not backing down. She demanded an apology, a sassy twelve-year-old trying to boss around a disturbed sixteen-year-old.

I just knew Cahir was about to fuck her up, so I stepped in between them trying to be a hero. Except Cahir laughed, apologized and told Rumor she was crazy as fuck. Rumor still appreciated my efforts, she smiled up at me, her hazel eyes shining, and I knew in that moment she was the one. Shorty was still young as fuck, so I kept her close to me. When I started hitting the streets, she would sneak out and sit on the block wit me all night. Rumor was the true definition of a good girl gone bad forever. I just knew our relationship would be unbreakable. But once a nigga got that big come up and went from moving eight balls to keys, I didn't want to be tied down. The money changed me, and the hood fame maimed me. I was all about new pussy and freak bitches. I forgot about the girl I loved. I just always thought she would be there when I was ready to settle down, waiting on a nigga.

The door to her room opened, and a nurse came out followed by my sister. "She still won't see you, Remee, I think you should just leave. I don't think she wants to see you again, ever. Just let her go." Amira's eyes were red and puffy from crying all night. I swear I couldn't comprehend what she was saying. I couldn't never see Rumor again, that wasn't how this shit was supposed to go.

"I need to know she is ok; I can't just leave." I was damn near yelling and people started to stare as they walked by. "The fuck you looking at," I growled to one of the security guards as he side-eyed me. "Move Amira, I'm going to see my girl, she needs me." My little sister wouldn't move; instead, she just gazed my way, her face filled with grief and pity.

"I told you, I warned you to stop fucking with all these bitches. Didn't I tell you karma was going to catch up to you? It didn't just catch up to you lil nigga, it caught up to Rumor." Cahir said as he walked up on me. He wasn't one of those loud niggas, he spoke in even tones, especially when he was mad. He slammed me up against the wall causing my head to snap back, I wasn't expecting that shit at all. "You need to leave. She doesn't need this right now. You think seeing you is going to make her feel better? Yo you selfish as fuck, you want to see her so you can feel better. Her son died, and she was damn near beat to death because you couldn't keep your dick in your pants. If Rumor wants to see you, she knows where to find you. If you want something to do, I left Jillian at the warehouse. Her friends are already chopped up and disposed of."

I wasn't scared of my cousin one fucking bit, my guns bust just like his. But what was the point of fighting back, everything he said was true. Pushing past him, I went to go and take my anger out on the girl who fucked up my entire world.

❧

I TRIED to stay away like everyone said, but I just couldn't. I spent the past twenty-four hours sitting in my truck just staring at the hospital like a fucking creep. Making the decision to go inside, I tucked my gun in my waist and made my way to the entrance. I almost missed her sitting there, but she was. Rumor didn't even look like the girl I knew. She was hunched over, staring into space as she sat on the bench. "Ru, what you doing out here ma," I asked low as I crouched down in front of her. Once Rumor noticed it was me, she physically cringed. That shit was like a bullet to the chest.

She was gone, I knew it in my heart after that shit. I saw it in the way she looked up at me. I could still picture the way her head was bleeding from the blows she took with the metal pipe. I knew she just wanted to get as far away from me as possible. Shit if I was her, I would have done the same thing. There were no words, I couldn't say anything to make this right. Do anything to make this ok. I had broken the only women I ever loved. I cost my son his life, and I had to live with that. She was shaking now, but there weren't any tears. Rumor was all cried out. "Come on ma, let me take you home. You can't be out here like this. Shit, you not even supposed to be doing all of this right now. I can't even believe these fucking people are letting you leave." I could barely look in her face at the bruises that would go from purple to blue then yellow in a few days.

"Remee, just go. I can't be around you right now," Rumor finally said, her voice shaking.

I just stood there watching her, wondering who she was waiting on. Did she call an Uber? Shit, I still had her car. "Ru, you ready," I heard a man call from behind me. I turned around to see my cousin stepping out of his blacked-out Audi and felt my blood boil.

"She good Cahir, I can drop her off wherever she is going." He didn't look bothered by me at all as he picked up her bag and held out his hand to help her up.

"Wouldn't make sense, she is staying with me until her apartment is ready. I'm sure you remembered that she didn't have a spot to lay her head."

I didn't waste time responding; instead, I punched this motherfucker in his face and kept swinging. "Nigga you thought my girl was coming home wit you? What you want to fuck her? I will kill you before I let that happen." I knew my cousin didn't want Rumor, but the shit didn't sit right with me. Why the fuck he would he want her to come home with him. She could come home with me, I could take care of her. I didn't want no other man around Rumor. I felt myself losing control and my cousin just let me get hit after hit off of him until I was damn near in tears. I couldn't bring my son back, I couldn't make Ru love me again. I felt like I had lost everything, and he was letting me take my anger out on him.

"A'Remee, stop," my mother screeched from the doorway of the hospital. A bunch of nosey motherfuckers were standing around looking, and Rumor was silently crying. Her hand fisted and held up to her mouth like she was trying to keep that shit inside. I stepped back and saw the blood on my fists. "Cahir, you knew better, so you deserved that. Rumor is going to Sire's house with Amira. Sire is not going to be there Remee so you can keep your fists to yourself. I would bring her home with me, but we all know you would be there day and night begging and to be honest its too late and I don't want to be a witness to it. I want you to leave this girl alone. A'Remee, leave her be!" My mother was crying, and I realized I didn't just hurt Rumor, but I had broken my mother's heart as well.

❧

I DID what my mother told me and stayed away from Rumor. Well, I at least stayed far enough away, so she didn't notice me. I sat in the back of the auditorium for her graduation in May. A lot of days I sat outside of her job and saw her through the glass windows. It didn't matter if she was folding clothes, or cashing people out I was still there, looking and missing my girl. I watched her struggle with the death of our son over the last few months, and that was the worst. Some days she would sit in her car and cry for hours before going inside her apartment. I hated that she lived in the projects and I made it clear to every nigga in the area she had better remain untouched and unharmed, or I was airing everyone out that bitch.

I sat in my tinted Benz and leaned the seat back. I parked in front of Rumor's apartments most nights and watched when she came home from work. I couldn't sleep anyway, so I had no problem sitting out here all night if I had to. I hit the blunt and let my head fall back as the smoke invaded my lungs. My hand unconsciously reached for the bottle of Henny that was already half gone. This was my new normal. If I wasn't handling business, I was getting fucked up. I closed my eyes, remembering how sweet Rumor's kisses were. How she would always bite on my bottom lip before sliding her tongue over it when I was dicking her down.

My thoughts were interrupted when my passenger side door flew open. I had my gun in my lap, but I didn't bother grabbing it when I smelled her perfume. It had been five months since we spoke. Five months since I was this close to Rumor. She looked even better up close. I noticed the dark circles around her eyes were finally gone, and even though she was frowning, she was still beautiful as hell. She had her legs out since she was wearing some little flowered maxi dress. "A'Remee we need to talk," she said, closing the door behind her and sitting down. I knew this wasn't no get back together type shit, so I didn't even bother getting happy. I hit the blunt again and nodded.

"What's good Ru?"

"You can't keep doing this. You sit out here every night, always at my job, posted up in front of the nail shop! It's some stalker shit, and I don't like it. Plus, I know this ain't good for you," she glanced at the bottle of liquor, and I saw the sadness in her eyes. "Listen, Rem, I want you to know I have forgiven you. I know you would have never intentionally put our son and me in harm's way. Could you have made better choices? We both know you could have. But I had to let go of the hate. It was tearing me up inside."

I grabbed her hand, causing an uncomfortable look to cover her face. "Rumor I never got to tell you this shit, but I'm truly sorry. I would die before I let someone hurt you and you know that. I just hope someday you can truly forgive me, that you can let me back in your life." If anything, she looked even more uncomfortable as she fidgeted in her seat.

"Remee, you have to let go, move on. Stop sitting out here, drinking your problems away. Stop sliding envelopes of money under my door." She snatched her hand back and went inside her purse. She started pulling out the white envelopes I would stuff with cash and slide under her door.

"Naw shorty don't do that. I've always taken care of you, nothing's changed. Don't even piss me off that way." She knew me enough to leave it alone. She put the money back in her bag and let out a sigh. Rumor was biting the hell out her bottom lip and pulling on her ear. So I knew there was more. "Ru I have known ya ass forever, so whatever it is, just say it."

"I met someone, I wanted to let you know before I made things official between us. That is why you have to move on. I don't want you waiting on me, because Remee, I'm not coming back." Shorty knocked the breath out of my body with this one. How the fuck she meet someone. We have barely been over a few months. I wanted to call her a hoe and a bitch, but I knew she wasn't. She was a woman scorned. I left her home alone damn near every night, while I fucked other girls. I never even gave her a title. So, I had to respect her moving on without me.

"Come on ma, stop biting ya lip and shit. I'm cool, I ain't about to fuck wit ya little ass. Come here right quick, though." I ashed the blunt and put my gun in the side of the door. I didn't think she was going to give in, but she slid over the console and straddled me. I swear her body fit perfect. "Just sit wit a nigga for a minute." She nodded and laid her head on my chest. I wanted to ride out and just kidnap her, take her home and lock her up until she loved me again.

It was silent in the car, for once my phones weren't ringing, probably because my attitude had been one of a savage lately and no one wanted to fuck wit me. I didn't even have the music on. I had my arms wrapped around Rumor, and I didn't know how the fuck I was going to let go. I felt her body relax, and I knew she had fallen asleep. I was trying not to move because I just wanted this shit to last forever. After a while, someone blew their car horn, causing her to jump up. "Rem, I have to go, it's getting late."

My heart stopped as I thought about this being it for me and Rumor. I had watched my pops die right in front of me, seen my son lifeless, not even fully formed, but this felt like the hardest thing I had ever done. I loosened my arms some. "Aight I just want to say something to you. If that nigga doesn't treat you good leave him the fuck alone. If he hurts you, I'm killing him, and don't try and hide that shit because I will know. Rumor, I just... Man, this shit is hard as fuck on a nigga." I ran my hand over my face and felt the tears I was trying to hide. "Just know I love you, like from the bottom of my heart, the depths of my soul love you." I felt like a bitch the way she had me feeling.

Instead of getting up, Rumor leaned forward and did that shit I loved with her tongue. I felt her soft lips on mine and my dick strained against my jeans. I let my tongue invade her mouth, and I felt her moan. My hands crept up her bare legs, once I got to her soft ass, I pulled her closer with one hand and undid my belt with the other. When she felt the head of my dick rubbing against the silk panties she had on, she hesitated. I knew I shouldn't be doing this, but if it was goodbye, I couldn't resist one last time.

I groaned when she pulled her panties to the side and slid down the length of me. She was so fucking wet, her pussy felt like home. Even though I fucked with a lot of girls, no one's pussy was as good as Rumors. She was trying to put in work, but I grabbed her hips and slowed her down. I wanted to enjoy every second with her. I trailed kisses up her neck then back down. I used my teeth to pull the straps to her dress down so I could get to her breasts. I took my time and sucked each one, I loved how her skin tasted sweet like honey. "Remee," she said, crying out my name. I knew she was about to cum and just like I thought I felt her clenching my dick. I couldn't hold out if I wanted to so I just let her milk the shit out of my dick.

I thought she was going to be filled with regret, but she didn't say a word. "Rumor promise me if you need me for anything you will let me know?"

"I promise," she said softly before she climbed off of me and fixed herself. She leaned over and kissed me on the cheek before getting out of the car, and just like that the woman I loved was walking away.

"BABY WHAT'S WRONG, you been in a bad mood all day," Jazmine asked as she rubbed my chest. I knocked her hands out of the way and grilled her. "Well fuck you then Remee. All I wanted was some dick. You've had a fucked-up attitude all week, and I'm tired of it." I swear this hoe was like three minutes from getting her throat slashed if she didn't shut the fuck up. This was what happened when I tried to move on. I got stuck with this annoying bitch. The head was good, and her ass was fat, but that was all she had going for her.

I ignored her whining and checked my watch. I was still undecided if I was going to Rumor's birthday dinner or not. My whole family still fucked with Rumor hard, and my mom and sister were hosting this shit for her. "Yo I got someplace to be so I will check you later." She jumped up like I threw boiling water on her.

Hands on her hips, she took the ratchet girl stance. "Where the hell you suddenly got to be?"

"It's some family shit, a birthday, even though it ain't none of your fucking business." I was wondering why I even came to this bitch's house today. I guess deep down I was trying to forget about not spending the day with Rumor. I wonder what her pussy ass man got for her. I made sure I found out who she was fucking with the same night she told me she was dating. I don't know where the fuck my baby girl found this busta ass dude from. He was out here getting a little bread in the streets. But he was a basic ass nigga at best.

"Can I come," Jazmine asked, her eyes wide like a child waiting for candy. My first thought was to say fuck no, but the more I thought about Rumor's man being there, I decided to say yes.

"Yo get dressed and be ready in an hour, or I'm leaving your ass. Don't put on no thot shit either we going to a nice restaurant." I left so I could go home and change clothes. I just prayed I could make it through the night without spilling anyone's blood. I pulled into my driveway and parked next to the for-sale sign. I decided to move after everything that happened. I should have never brought any bitches to where I laid my fucking head. I jogged up the stairs and walked into my closet. I decided on a pair of Balmain jeans, a white and red Polo shirt and a pair of white Gucci sneakers and a white Gucci belt. I got in the shower and washed my ass, then got dressed. Throwing on my iced-out Jesus piece, diamond bracelet and Rolex I sprayed on my Gucci Guilty and made sure I grabbed an extra nine.

On the way to my truck, I grabbed the sparkly gift bags and balloons I had by the door. I smoked a blunt to the head on the way to Jazmine's house, trying to calm my damn nerves. I wasn't ready to see my girl with another nigga. As soon as I pulled up to this bitch's house, she was out the door without me even having to call. Looks like she was waiting by the window for a nigga. I wasn't surprised, all these bitches were trying to roll wit my family. She opened the passenger side door and rolled her eyes. I knew she didn't think I was doing that shit for her, this definitely wasn't that.

We pulled up to Mortons, and I handed the valet my keys. She seemed satisfied that he opened the door for her. At least she cleaned up nice, she had on a black dress that hugged her fake body in all the right places. Her long straight weave was pulled up into some fancy looking bun with a sparkly clip that matched her earrings. Walking in, I felt like all eyes were on me. Amira was being a drama queen standing there with her mouth wide open, staring at Jazmine. Ignoring her, I dapped my brother and cousin up and then hugged my mom. The whole time I couldn't keep my eyes off of Rumor. She was sitting at the head of the table looking fly as fuck. She was rocking a scrunchy silky looking purple and cream dress. She had on her Tiffany jewelry I had copped her, and her natural hair was wavy and flowing down her back. The most beautiful girl in the fucking world.

I stepped to her, forgetting all about Jazmine. "Happy Birthday ma," I said as I hugged her. I probably held on to her longer than I should have, but I didn't give a fuck. I noticed her nigga wasn't here yet; hopefully he would stay where the fuck he was at. I set her gift bags and shit on the floor next to her and stepped back. My mom elbowed me and cut her eyes at my guest. "This Jazmine. Jazmine this is Rumor, she is the birthday girl, this is my mom and my sister and everybody else." She smiled and gave a little girly wave. I knew her ass was feeling special right now, but she wasn't. I sat down and motioned for her to sit next to me. Turning my attention back to Rumor, I gave her a smile. "Open ya gifts girl."

"Later Rem, I want to eat first." I nodded and flagged down the waitress. My mom had rented the whole restaurant for tonight, so it was just us. For the first time, I realized Rumor didn't have a bunch of friends. She had her one female cousin here, and everyone else was my people. I was sure that had something to do with me. The food was good as fuck and Rumor seemed happy, except when she would look at her phone every so often and send a text. Her face would frown up, and I noticed her pushing the sadness to the back. I had a feeling it was her so-called man ruining her special day. He should have been here, and I know for a fact he was invited because my mom warned me, he would be in attendance. I was cool with the fact that he wasn't here. I mean fuck him. But I didn't like him hurting baby girl.

"Ok, we are going to sing happy birthday and cut the cake. Then Rumor can get to her gifts," my mom directed. After we ate the sweet ass cake my baby started opening up her presents. My sister got her some sister bracelet and tickets to see Beyoncé in concert. I was sure I paid for that shit too. Sire and Cahir gave her new purses with cash in them, and my mom gave her a spa day for her, my mom and sister. When she finally got to the bags, I gave her she slowly peered inside the first one. She pulled out the teddy bear and smiled so hard I could see all her teeth. I copped shorty everything I thought she could want, a new iPhone, a trip to Miami for her and Amira, a few racks, some Gucci outfits and Gucci sneakers. When she picked up the last box, she held it in her hands for a minute and just stared.

Finally, she lifted it up and revealed the diamond-encrusted key pendant. One tear rolled down her cheek before she undid the clasp and put it on. "Thank you, Rem, I love it." She gave me a teary-eyed smile before she got up and started gathering all her gifts.

"What the fuck Remee, are you fucking this girl or something?" Jazmine hissed from the other side of me.

"Man shut the fuck up yo. You invited yourself to this shit so don't ask me nothing." I gave her a warning look as I got up so we could leave. We all headed out at the same time, and I noticed Jordan's bitch ass walking up to Rumor. This nigga really showed up to her dinner after the shit was done. I tried not to pay attention to shit they had going on as I waited on the valet to get my truck.

"Where the hell were you Jordan, you knew what time my dinner started," Rumor snapped.

"Girl don't be stressing me, I fucking told you I had business to take care of. I will take you out tomorrow or some shit. It's just a birthday."

"Yo, you not about to go check that nigga," Sire asked as he came and stood next to me. I didn't even respond, just stared straight ahead. That was exactly what I was trying not to do, was check this dude.

"So tell me something Rumor, who the fuck bought you this shit?" He had the necklace I bought her in his hand and a scowl on his face. He turned to look my way before focusing back on Rumor. "Oh, so this nigga buying you gifts and shit. I bet you still fucking him too. I knew ya ass was a hoe the way you gave me the pussy after a few dates." Rumor was standing there looking crushed. I expected her to pop off on his ass, but instead, she was just silent.

"Sir, your car is here," the valet said, handing me my keys.

"Jazmine, go wait in the truck and don't bring your ass out

here." She rolled her eyes but climbed in the truck and closed the door. I walked over to Rumor and her supposed man. "Yo, is it a fucking problem over here? Ru you good?"

"Naw nigga ain't no fucking problem, why don't you go worry about ya bitch while I worry about mine." See I knew someone was going to end up bloody as fuck before the night was over. I grabbed my nine and went upside his head with it. I wanted to peel his fucking cap back, but this wasn't the time or place.

"Don't you ever call her a bitch again, and I know it ain't no fucking problem because it's time for yo ass to step." He held his bloody face and backed away. I knew this wasn't over, I could see it in his eyes. But at least he made the best decision for himself tonight. "Aight Ru, be good ma." I went and hopped in my truck and peeled out.

Jazmine tried to hold a conversation, but I shut it the fuck down. I turned the music up and sped the whole way to her crib. Pulling up, I popped the lock and mugged her until she got out. I never even waited for her to get in the house just pulled the fuck off. I ended up exactly where I knew I was going to, the projects. Rumor's car was already there in her parking spot, but I decided to wait a while before I went inside. I sat in the truck drinking Patron straight to the head and smoking back to back. Just knowing this dude, she was with was treating her worse than I ever did had me stressed the fuck out.

I got out and stumbled inside, I was happy as fuck shorty lived on the first floor, so it was only a short ass flight of stairs before I got to her door. I knocked loud as fuck, not caring that it was three in the morning. Slowly she cracked the door open, seeing her puffy eyes had me not even waiting for her to invite me in. I pushed the door open and took her in my arms. Instead of pushing me away, she wrapped her arms around me. I locked the door and turned to look down and Rumor. "What are you doing here, Rem? Are you drunk?"

"Shit I just didn't like how you looked earlier. I wanted to

make sure you were good. And yea ma, I'm fucked up for real."
Shit, I had been drinking since dinner.

"Come sleep that shit off," she said as she pulled out of my
arms and walked towards the back of the tiny apartment. I
couldn't help but watch her ass jiggle in her lime green boy
shorts. "How you gonna come here not knowing if my man was
here, or on his way. Shit, he could be living wit me or
something."

I took my jewelry off and set it on her bedside table,
followed by both of my guns. Stripping down to my boxers and
my wife-beater I got in her bed. "Come to bed Rumor, I need
some pussy and some sleep. And I ain't worried about that nigga
living here or coming over. You not about to have some new
dude in your space like that. Shit, you never even slept overnight
with another nigga besides me."

She laughed and turned out the lights. "I guess you right or
whatever. And you are welcome to get as much sleep as you
want, but the pussy is a no." I pulled her close to me, and my
hand found its way to her honey pot. She was dripping and got
even wetter once I touched her. I rubbed her clit until I felt her
shudder. I stripped her before she could tell me no and laid her
on her back. I wanted to see her face while I fucked her.
"Remee, stop, I have a man," she whined, but I kissed her so she
wouldn't say shit else. I wasn't trying to hear about the pussy ass
motherfucker.

I never got any sleep, I made love to Rumor all night long.
After our third round, she passed out in my arms, and I just laid
there watching her sleep until the sun came up. Gently kissing
her on her forehead, I got up and rolled out while she was still
sleeping. I didn't want to wait around for her to tell me how she
had a man or how she wasn't fucking wit me. My heart couldn't
take that.

7

ARABELLA

I WATCHED Alex pace the room in front of me, his dick swinging, still covered in my juices. He ran his hand over his perfect waves as he made a sound that was in between a laugh and a roar. "Arabella, I thought you understood, no I know you understood that I was to be your first. I waited a long time for this. I invested a lot of money into this household just for this pleasure. But for some reason you let someone take that from me." He slammed me against the wall, suddenly causing my whole body to scream in pain. I didn't see that coming, he had lived with us for almost seven years, and I had never seen him get violent. But I guess it was always just below the surface, something in the way he spoke to my mother and my sister that should have warned me. I felt the blows to the side of my head and my ribs as he rained down punches everywhere, he could.

"Who is he?" he yelled in my face, but I just shook my head. I wasn't getting Sire caught up in my bullshit. For a second, I wondered if he had already forgotten about me. We had texted back and forth for a few days, but I was scared that Alex and my mother would somehow find out, so I blocked his number. It was for the best, he was pretty clear on the fact he didn't do the whole girlfriend thing. I remember feeling relief flood my body when he said that. I knew I had to let him go, and that made it easier. He gave me an out. "Your nothing but a lying bitch, from now on you only go to school and home. I'm having your phone cut off, and when I find out who took my prize, I'm killing him." He dropped me in a broken heap on my bedroom floor before he turned to go back into his room. I hate it here. I had to find a way to get out.

TRUE TO HIS WORD, Alex had my phone turned off and made sure I couldn't go anywhere but school and home. He made sure of this because he picked me up from school instead of letting me take the bus. Watching me had become his fulltime job. It had been three months since he started having sex with me, and it was worse than my sister described. He made sure to bite me all over my body, causing me to bleed and have marks. He would spank my ass so hard his handprints were left behind for days. In that time, I had developed a deep hatred for my mother, who has turned a blind eye to the situation. I was sure she noticed her man was never in her bed at night; instead, he was in mine. When I couldn't take the pain, I would close my eyes and pretend Sire was coming to save me. I never took off the charm bracelet he gave me, and it was the only thing that gave me joy these days.

I paced my room like a caged animal, I didn't even get to go to school today since last night got out of control. Instead of some bites and bruises, I ended up with a black eye and handprints on my neck. I shouldn't have fought Alex back, but when he thought I was going to give him head, I lost it. I knew sooner than later he was going to kill me because I wasn't my sister, and this couldn't be my life. "Take the fuckin trash out Bella, since your ass stuck in this house all day," my mother snapped. I wanted to jump on her wrinkled faced ass so bad. Like bitch, I'm home because your man was violating me. Kissing my teeth, I got up to take out the trash. It was the closest to freedom I was going to get today.

I threw the bags in the green cans and leaned on the porch for a few minutes. Lately, I felt sick most of the day, and the fresh air was doing me some good. I jumped some when the black on black Benz screeched to a stop in front of my house. If the ride wasn't so nice, I would have thought it was a drive-by. The driver's door opened, and like a vision, Sire was climbing out. "Yo shorty where the fuck you been?" He said as he jogged over to me. I didn't know what to say, but luckily, he wrapped me in his arms, so I didn't have to say anything, yet.

I hugged him back, letting my face fall into his chest and breath in his cologne. I let out a small sigh before I finally let go. "You didn't answer, I been calling you and shit, but it says your phone is off. If you needed some bread, you could have said something." I just shook my head, money for a phone bill wouldn't have helped my situation.

"Nothing like that, I just had a lot going on." I dropped my head only for him to grab my chin and lift it up. I saw his face change, and I remembered the marks on my neck and face.

"Arabella, who the fuck is putting they hands on you?" His grip on my chin tightened, and I could feel how angry he was. My eyes shifted to the house behind me before I looked up at him.

"No one is, I'm good Sire. But I should be getting back in the house." I knew someone would be coming out to look for me soon. "It was good to see you, I really missed you." I heard my voice, and it sounded shaky as fuck.

"Is it somebody in there? And don't fucking lie, I can clearly see somebody fucking you up. Matter of fact you want to leave right now. Get your stuff, I got you Bells." I could tell he meant it too. I thought about just leaving, I didn't even need anything from inside. All this house had was bad memories and a lot of pain.

"Aww isn't this cute?" My sister said sarcastically as she

walked up with a scowl on her face. As soon as I saw her, I knew it was about to be some shit. Since I spent my birthday weekend with Sire, she had been treating me like her worst fucking enemy. I wasn't stupid, I realized she was mad I had someone she wanted. "Little sister I'm sure Alex wouldn't be happy to see you out here talking to some man." Her voice held a warning tone, and I knew I had to get the fuck inside now before I ended up with another black eye.

"Hey bitch, when I saw yo ass a few weeks ago, you told me Bella moved out of town, and you hadn't seen her since. The fuck you lying for? I hope you didn't think I was ever fucking wit you, I don't care if shorty was on the fucking moon." She laughed evilly as she slowly backed towards the stairs. Shrugging she went to turn around, but Sire grabbed her arm so hard she fell on her ass. "I don't fucking play games shorty, run me the fucking money I gave you for Bella before I split your shit wide open." My head shot up, money. *What the fuck?*

"Sire, I ain't got it all, I swear I was going to give it all to her. I just needed some of it for an emergency, you know how it is. Let me run in the house and get what I have for you," she begged. He grabbed his gun from his waist and nodded for her to go and get his bread. I watched her scramble to her feet, not even brushing the dirt off of her pants.

"Sire, why did you give her money?" I asked once she disappeared behind the screen door.

"Shit, I gave her the money for you. I told her I needed to know where you were, and she said you went away to some school out of state. Told me some story about how you couldn't even eat because your parents wouldn't send you any funds. I told her to make sure you called me and gave her a couple of hundred so you could buy some food and shit." I could tell he was pissed, Keke had that effect on people. She had started scheming a lot of niggas lately, and one of these days it was going to catch up to her. Shit today might just be the day.

I felt my chest get tight just knowing he was willing to help me out even after I ghosted him. "You didn't have to do that Sire, but it was sweet of you." I leaned up to kiss him on the cheek, but he turned his head, and I ended up kissing his lips.

"I ain't got to do shit baby girl, but I don't mind for you." His voice was serious, and I knew he meant what he said. I wished I had met him at a different time in my life, one that would have allowed me to explore my feelings for him. He gently grabbed my arm, his hand caressing the bare skin until he made it to my bracelet. "You still be wearing this shit, huh?" He questioned. Before I could respond, I heard a door slam behind me, causing me to jump and him to look up.

"Nigga who the fuck are you," Alex barked as he damn near ran down the stairs in nothing but a wife-beater and a pair of boxers. I could see Keke standing on the porch with a smirk on her face. That bitch. "Arabella get the fuck inside, now," he snapped as he went to snatch me up.

"Yo pussy fuck you, she ain't going nowhere." Sire moved me behind him and had his gun out. "The better question is who the fuck are you, since this my girl. You look a little old to be trying to fuck with her anyway, so you need to take your ass back in the house. Old ass nigga."

"Look I don't care about all that shit your talking. This is my stepdaughter and when I say move, she better fucking move. That's why her face look like that now, little ass don't listen. I already called the police, and they are on the way, so the best thing for you to do is head out." I felt my heart sink when he said the police were on the way, he was a punk, so I'm sure he was telling the truth. I could see by the way Sire was about to run up on him he didn't give a fuck about the pigs. But I couldn't let him get into trouble, especially for me.

I jumped in front of him and put my hands on his chest. "Sire, just leave, please. I don't want you to get in trouble. It isn't worth it, I'm not worth it." I let the tears I had been holding spill over onto my cheeks. He used the back of his hand to wipe them away. "I swear I will be ok, I don't want you getting locked up. I love you too much for that," I said, damn near whispering the last part. I could tell by the way his eye color changed slightly, he heard me.

"Bells if you need me, anytime ma just call. I will come for you anytime, anywhere. Your more than worth it and I always got you shorty." He pointed his gun at Alex one more time before he started to back up some. "Hold this," he said, reaching in his pocket and handing me some money. "Remember what the fuck I said, you better come find a nigga if you need me, I ain't hard to find ma." He kissed my forehead before glaring at my sneaky ass sister. "Bitch anytime I see you it's on site, jealous ass." I watched as he got in his car and peeled off my heart breaking.

"So that's the little nigga you let get my pussy," Alex hissed as I slinked into the house. I had never felt this low, I should have just run off with Sire when he first pulled up. I ignored everything Alex was saying and went to get a bottle of water. I thought about the bottle of Aspirin in the medicine cabinet, and I considered taking the whole thing. I glanced at the kitchen knives and wondered was I strong enough to stab Alex to death. Feeling a strong arm on my shoulder, I looked up into the face of my own personal devil. "You will pay for this, now go and put on something sexy. You have a lot of making up to do."

I ran out of the room, feeling my stomach bubble at the thought of him. I swear this throwing up shit was daily and getting old fast. I made it to the bathroom just in time and threw up everything I ate for breakfast and lunch. "Wow, I guess Alex wasn't careful with you. He always used condoms with me. Now you're stuck with him forever." Keke stood there giggling, her hands on her hips. I never knew my sister could be so cruel. She was older than me. She was supposed to protect me, but I guess it didn't fit into her agenda. "Well little sis, if you want me to give Petey a call I'm sure he will be willing to help you with some abortion money." I felt like she had slapped me in the face when she said abortion, I hadn't even thought about being pregnant, but in that moment, I knew for sure I was.

"Who is getting an abortion," Alex boomed from the hallway. I swear there was no privacy in this fucking house. His face was twisted, and his eyes had a look I couldn't decipher. "Who's pregnant?"

"Arabella is, I was just offering her some options," Keke said. Alex's hand went across her face so fast it made me flinch.

"Don't ever try and get rid of my blessings." He turned to me suddenly and caressed my face. I wanted to puke all over again from his touch. Hell, I thought he was the reason I was throwing up all the time anyway, the thought of him near me immediately made me sick. "Our baby," he cooed while rubbing my still flat belly. "Go relax Arabella. I will bring you some tea and toast to settle your stomach." Something in his smile was off as fuck. I felt my skin crawl, and I just wanted to disappear. Instead, I ran out of the bathroom. I made sure to bump the shit out of my sister as I did. I wanted to beat her ass right this second, but I hope she knew once I could, I was fucking her up.

⚜

"BELLA, you sure you want to do this?" My best friend asked looking at me with concern. I felt the smoothness of the shiny paper as my thumb brushed over the image of my baby girl. As soon as the doctor said you're having a girl, I knew what I had to do. I would die before I ever allowed my daughter to go through what I was. I looked in the backseat of Eternity's car at my duffel bag and suitcase and shook my head.

"I'm sure." I was leaving today one way or another. I climbed out of the car into the stifling heat and wished I could have come to look for Sire at an indoor venue. But time was of the essence, and I knew he would be here. His family was hosting this block party, so it was damn near a guarantee. I smoothed the front of my flowery maxi dress and rested my hand on my belly for a moment. "Mommy is going to figure this out," I whispered.

"Ooh girl, let's get this over with. It's too hot to have all these black folks in one spot. I feel the waves of heat and funk coming off these niggas." Eternity was fanning herself with her hand and being her usual dramatic self. "Come on bestie, let me buy you a slushy or some fried Oreos," she offered like she was reading my mind. After getting some treats and walking further into the crowd, I spotted Sire. Even though I hadn't seen him in months, there was no missing him. He was looking sexy as always, with his white Armani shorts, white and navy Armani tee and all of his bling he was shitting on the rest of these niggas.

"There he goes," I said nudging Eternity.

"Girl, you sure he not the daddy? That nigga is fine as fuck, he could have taken my virginity too. He could have had whatever he wanted." She laughed, causing me to giggle. I knew she was playing, but he really was fine as fuck. "What you waiting on, go get your man. He said anytime you needed him, and he looks like a nigga who keeps his word."

She was right. Slowly I waddled, my new version of walking since this, big ass baby had me fucked up. Right before I got to him, a skinny girl with a red bob came up next to him and wrapped her arms around his waist. At the same time, he looked up, and his eyes met mine. Not wanting to see him and his newest girl any longer I turned and damn near ran the other way.

"Damn you move fast for a pregnant girl," Eternity said as she jogged to catch up to me. "Why didn't you go talk to him. He was calling out to you, Bella."

"It's too late. He's moved on, and what did I expect. No one was about to wait around on my ass forever, or come and rescue me like Cinderella. This ain't no fucking fairytale, this is my life. And no, I still ain't going back, I'm going to figure this shit out." I had no idea where my baby and I were going, but I knew it wasn't back to Alex's house of horrors. I knew I could figure this shit out, I had to.

❁ 8 ❁
SIRE

"Son aint that the bitch you took to your crib a while back, the one with the fat ass?" Remee said nodding his head into the crowd of people. I hated these parties, shit I felt like I needed security to beat these sketchy hoes the fuck off of me. It took me a minute to search the sea of thots surrounding my family but I finally spotted her. She looked beautiful just like always. For a second I remembered the bruises all over her the last time I saw her and felt a wave of anger come over me. I wanted to go back for her, I thought about it everyday since then but I could see her stepfather and sister would do anything to send a nigga to prison. And me being locked up wasn't going to help the situation.

"Yea that's shorty, don't be calling her no fucking bitch either," I snapped in response.

Remee raised an eyebrow, "looks like she has something to tell you. Did you strap up?" I noticed her belly out in front of her as she got closer to me. She looked tired, and I remembered telling her to come and find me if she ever needed anything. Shit, if it was my baby I wasn't going to act a fool about the situation. I wasn't careful and I knew better, she really didn't.

"Man, mind ya fucking business." I went to step forward so I

66

could meet her halfway and some chick I dicked down a few times jumped in my face. She put her arms around my neck causing my head to snap back.

"Yo, bitch get the fuck up off a me," I barked shoving the random from in front of me. As I pushed her off I saw Bella turn the other way and damn near run through the park. I called her name but she just kept it moving. I already knew what was up, Marcella's retarded ass approached me like I was her fucking man. I couldn't make it through the crowd without someone stopping to talk to me and by the time I got anywhere Arabella was long gone.

"Marcella come here," I said as I walked back to were Remee and Cahir were posted up. She was so fucking awestruck just to be in my presence, even when I called her out her name and damn near shoved her down. "Bitch you just fucked up some shit thats important to me," I raged grabbing her by the neck. Before I could snap her shit Remee was there stopping me, his hand on my shoulder. Lucky for her because I wasn't about to stop.

"Bro, let her ass go, what the fuck is wrong with you? Since when you get all bent out of shape about one of these hoes? It's like you trying to go to jail over some pussy." I shrugged out of his grip and grilled him.

"Fuck you Remee, I don't say shit when you be out here dropping niggas and bitches for Rumor! You don't know shit about ole girl or what me and her have going on. She aint like the rest of thes girls." I rarely got into it with my brother but, since he felt like him being a few years older than me meant he ran my life I was about to be on some fuck you shit. "Fuck this shit I'm out."

I made my way through the park until I got to my Ferarri. Hopping in I backed out of the spot and sped across town. I went to the house I last saw Bella at hoping she went back there. The threat of going to jail no longer crossing my mind. I would just get rid of her people if I had to. I jumped out of the car and banged on the door. No one answered or moved inside and after

I while I gave up. Shit maybe she was still at the park somewhere. I hoped she didn't have no other nigga in her face. That would piss me off, and I was already on edge. I didn't feel like being around anybody so I just drove to the crib and poured a drink. I always thought about Arabella, when I was fucking other girls I wished they were her. Shit if anything she was the first person I thought of when I woke up in the morning. I even bought groceries once to stock up my kitchen, hoping I could bring her over to cook. She was so fucking sweet and innocent, I wanted to show her the world, to protect her from evyerone, and most of all just keep her up under me.

❦

I RODE by Arabella's crib every week for the last few months and no one ever came to the door. Today someone was answering this mother fucker or I was going in. My patience about the situation was gone. I parked down the street and watched the house for a little while, hoping I could catch her going in or out. When the sun went down I put on my black gloves and went to knock one more time. No one came to the door so I jogged to the yard and broke the window in the back door. I wasn't about to waste time trying to pick no fucking locks. Searching the house, my heart sank when I realized it was pretty much empty.

I waited too long to come for her, I felt like she really needed me. She wouldn't have come looking for me otherwise. Bella could have been the one. And even if she wasn't, I still cared about her enough to want her to be straight. Her hoe ass sister hadn't been out since before the block party. But I was still keeping my eyes opened for her. If I had to kidnap Keke to find Bella I would. She could get tortured and all. Heading back to my car I couldn't believe that I had caught feelings for a girl after one weekend. Or that I let her slip away. I knew that no matter how many bitch's I came across none of them would ever compare to her.

❧ 9 ❧

RUMOR

I FELT someone shove my shoulder hard as fuck causing me to groan. I hated being woken up, plus the dream I was having was a good one. "Really, Rumor? You calling out that nigga's name in your sleep and shit. I'm tired of this if you want that nigga go be with him because I ain't coming second to no one, not even Remee McKenzie." Jordan sat up in the bed next to me talking shit early as fuck. I did feel a little guilty because I had no idea that the dream I had about Remee would be revealed to my man. I wondered was it the first time I had cried out for Remee in my sleep.

I shrugged at Jordan as I struggled to sit up. It seemed like my baby bump had turned into a huge belly almost overnight. Lately, Remee had been on my mind more and more even though I hadn't seen him in months. I made it a point to avoid him because I knew me being pregnant by another man would hurt him. I was still trying to wrap my head around this shit. Jordan and I had only been together for six months when I found out. And even though I would never regret my baby, the daddy was a whole other story. I jumped into something with him to try and get over my one true love, except now I felt like the universe was laughing at me. Because if anything being with another nigga, one who could never measure up to Remee was the opposite of what I was going for.

"I have a doctor's appointment at eleven, are you coming?" I asked, my voice hopeful. We were finding out what we were having today, and even though Jordan made no effort to attend any other appointments, I figured he would make an effort for this one.

"Ask that nigga Remee to go with you. I'm out." He stood up and stomped to the bathroom to get dressed. I sat back and closed my eyes, trying not to scream. Dealing with this nigga was like dealing with a bad ass child. I kept my eyes closed until I heard the front door to my apartment slam. I shot Amira a text letting her know she could come to the ultrasound appointment with me. At least someone was interested in being there. Amira was so excited to become a Godmother I would have had to beat her with a stick to keep her away.

I ate breakfast and went to handle my hygiene. It was cold outside, so I threw on a grey sweatsuit I had from Fashion Nova and some tall yellow rain boots. By the time I pulled my long hair back into a braid down my back, I was tired all over again. Grabbing my black puffer coat, I walked outside. I swear I felt more pregnant than the doctors said I was. It didn't take long for me to pull into the hospital lot and park. Amira was standing at the door impatiently moving from side to side, causing me to giggle. "Mira, you act like I'm carrying your baby," I said as I gave her a hug.

"Well I mean you kind of are, we gonna share this baby because I don't want to fuck up my body carrying one. Plus I plan to spoil and send baby back home."

"Thanks," I replied dry as hell. We walked inside, and I signed in. I was anxious about this pregnancy after losing my son. I barely left my house most days, I had even stopped working. I was living off of the money that Remee insisted on still leaving every few weeks. Jordan never questioned how I was surviving and barely offered to pay anything. It really just depended on his mood.

"Hello Miss Frances, follow me." The nurse instructed. As we walked down the hall to the back, I caught a whiff of cologne, and it made me think of Remee. He always wore that scent, Gucci Guilty. I must have been losing it. I hopped up on the table and said a prayer that my baby was ok. As the nurse tried to close the door, it was being pushed open from the other side.

"Shit my bad, I'm late, I had trouble finding the room," Remee said as he strolled in like he belonged. He looked good as fuck like always. His dreads were in a ponytail on the top of his head, and he had in his platinum grill. I gave him a confused look because I had no idea what he was doing here. But he just ignored it. The nurse gave him a lust-filled look and stepped back, letting him come inside further.

"I'm sorry I thought the father wasn't able to make it today." I felt like her ass just wanted to speak to him, she never had to say all of that. I cut my eyes Amira's way, but she looked just as surprised as I did.

Before I could tell her, he wasn't the father he nudged Amira some and sat down next to me. "Naw I made it. I will always find a way for my baby." I was grilling the shit out of him and praying that Jordan didn't decide to pop up. I didn't need this type of stress. Remee leaned over and whispered in my ear. "Calm down shorty, the fuck you looking all jumpy for. That other nigga can't whoop me."

I waited for the nurse to turn her attention to the machine before I responded. "Remee, what the hell are you doing here," I hissed. "This isn't your baby, you know I would have told you if it was," I said, sadly remembering the way he fucked me to sleep on the night of my Birthday.

Slowly he nodded, I could see in his eyes he thought it might have really been his. But he had to know me better than that. "Ma, this still my fucking baby. And I ain't missing none of the important shit so just chill." I sat back and looked to Amira for help, but she shrugged. I guess she wasn't interested in dealing with her brother's crazy today. He gripped my hand, and I felt myself relax a little.

"This is going to be cold," the nurse said as she squirted the gel onto my belly. A few seconds later, I heard my baby's heartbeat fill the room. "Ok do you want to know what you're having today." Amira, Remee, and I all said yes at the same time.

She moved the probe around some and clicked a bunch of buttons. "Looks like you are having a little girl. Congratulations." I felt my stomach being wiped clean and watched as she printed some of the ultrasound pictures. She handed them to us before leaving the room. I didn't know how I felt, kind of numb, I guess. I was happy it wasn't a boy because no one would be able to replace the son I lost. But I had no idea how to take care of a little girl, be a good mother to a little girl. My mother definitely didn't give me any examples to follow.

"Well I will see you two later because I have to start buying baby stuff," Amira said as she moved closer to the door. "Rem, call Amex, so they don't question the charges." She smirked and damn near ran out. I felt bad for Remee at this point because his sister was about to go spend all his bread on my baby. To make it worse he picked up his phone and called them in front of me, informing them that he was approving large purchases on the other card on his account.

"A'Remee, don't let her buy a lot of stuff for this baby. First of all, I don't need it. Second of all, I have nowhere to put it all. Remember my place is small."

I went to pull my shirt down to cover my belly, but his strong hand covered mine. Gently he touched my belly, and I felt my baby girl kick. "Don't worry, baby girl daddy is going to give you the world," he said as he talked to my belly, clearly ignoring what the fuck I said. I didn't know what the hell had gotten into Remee, maybe he had lost his mind. Did my pregnancy push him over the edge? "Come on, my mom is making that French toast you like." So that was how he knew about the baby and my appointments. I should have known Miss Layla would say something. I got my stuff together so I could go get a plate of food, I wasn't turning down any meals these days.

THE BANGING at my door caused the textbook I was studying to fall onto the floor. Great, now my fat ass had to find a way to bend and pick it up. "Coming," I shouted as I got up to see who I was about to curse out for beating on my fucking door like the police. Flinging the door open I was shoved so hard I fell against the side table I kept my mail on. "What the fuck is wrong with you, Jordan!" I shouted. He stood in front of me, his light brown skin flushed red, his juicy lips in a straight line. Since I found out I was having a girl, me and Jordan's relationship had become strained. I basically been going through the second half of my pregnancy alone at a time I expected him to put in more effort, start making plans on providing for our daughter and me. But all he wanted to do was fuck, get a home-cooked meal and run the streets.

"BITCH, WHY THE FUCK THIS NIGGA NAMING CLUBS AND SHIT AFTER YOU?" He was yelling at me like I was his fucking child. His eyes were snapping, and I knew he was angry, but I didn't know why.

"First off watch how the fuck you're talking to me. And what kind of man pushes his pregnant girlfriend? You better not ever put your fucking hands on me again. And I have no idea what club you're talking about. In case you didn't notice, I don't go out much these days." I cut my eyes at him before turning to go back to the couch. I was over Jordan, and if he kept this shit up, I wasn't calling Remee, I was going to call Cahir, and then Jordan's family could pick up whatever was left of his body when he was done with him. I eyed the lamp next to me and felt the urge to pick it up and smash his head in. He had the right fucking one today.

"Listen, my bad for pushing you. But you need to tighten shit up. I'm tired of you and this nigga playing me. And stop fucking lying saying you don't know what's going on. The whole fucking city is talking about the new club, Rumours! He naming clubs and shit after you and you swear ya'll not still fucking? You need to call him and tell him to name his fucking club something else, and you not going to that baby shower his family giving you. You need to stop spending time with them, they not ya peoples. I will have my mom throw you a little baby shower or whatever. I wonder if this is even my damn baby." He was standing over me like I was moved by his presence. The fact that he suddenly wanted to deny our child had me looking at him with disgust.

"Jordan, you need to leave until you not coming at me on this disrespectful shit. I have not even met your mother. And the family of yours I did meet couldn't stand me. I ain't giving up my special day because you're insecure over a nigga I don't fuck wit anymore. You are acting like a real bitch right now, just get out."

"Man fuck you. If you go to that baby shower, just know I'm going with your hoe ass." Instead of leaving like I requested, he stormed off to the bedroom and slammed the door. I hated dealing with this stupid mother fucker I really did. Rubbing my hand over my stomach, I tried to calm my daughter down. She was moving around fucking up my insides. Sighing I decided to call Remee.

I had never deleted his contact or blocked him when we broke up. I scrolled to his name that still had heart emojis next to it and clicked call. It rang twice before he picked it up. "Ru you and my baby good?" I rolled my eyes. I had told him several times over the past few months that he had to stop saying shit like that. No wonder my man was in here going the fuck off.

"Rem, we talked about this. But that's not why I called. I umm heard about the club your opening. I'm really proud of you, I know that was something you always talked about doing. But I need you to change the name." The line got quiet, and I had to look and make sure he didn't hang up.

Finally, he chuckled low, and I could picture him running his hand over his face. He always did that shit when he was frustrated. "Ru, I opened that club for you. Because I wanted to make sure if I don't make it out of these streets you and baby girl got something solid, legal to make sure ya'll straight. Don't ever come asking me no dumb shit because ya nigga can't handle it. If he wants the name changed, tell him to make me change that shit and leave you out of it. I told you no man in your life was ever going to stop shit that me, and you got going on. I'm always going to be ya nigga and you always going to be my number one."

I didn't even know how to respond. I swear this nigga had lost his fucking mind and I wasn't beat for this shit. "Rem, I don't know what to even say, you just do what the fuck you want." I heard movement from the bedroom, and I knew I had to end the call. "Just think about what I said, please. I have to go."

❧

I LOOKED in the mirror and smiled. The wand curls that Amira just finished had me looking like an exotic princess. I don't know where she found a dress this pretty to fit my fat pregnant behind, but I was grateful. The rose-pink material was filled with what looked like Swarovski crystals, and the bottom flared out into rows of lace tulle. My slippers were also rose-colored with crystals. "Ooh Rumor if you cry and mess up your make-up, I'm going to fuck you up. Now hold still so I can add the tiara and we will be done." I sniffed back the tears because Amira sounded serious about fucking me up.

Hearing clapping behind me, I looked in the mirror to see Jordan staring at me with hate in his eyes. He didn't say a word, just stood there slow clapping like a hoe. I tried to ignore him, but it was embarrassing that he was acting like this in front of my company. "So, I guess you going, huh?" He questioned as he finally stopped trying to put on a show.

"Why the fuck wouldn't she be going to her baby shower? Is there a problem?" Amira sassed, reaching towards her purse. Lord, I prayed she didn't shoot him in my bedroom. I wasn't in the mood or shape to clean up the blood. "I guess you can't hear now. But yea she is going, you should be grateful someone is looking out for your girl and kid." I knew she wanted to say more, but luckily, she didn't. I tried my best not to talk about my relationship with anyone because I knew Jordan's blood would most likely be on my hands. I wasn't sure if Remee would still kill for me since we weren't together anymore, but I didn't want to take the chance.

"Ok, Mira, I'm ready. Can you carry my bag please?" She grabbed my duffel with comfy clothes in case I wanted to change later and grilled Jordan as we headed out. He pouted as he followed me into the hallway so I could lock up. He was probably annoyed he would have to spend the day at his mama's house. But I didn't trust him enough to give him a key to my shit, plus it wasn't like he paid any of the bills here. I tried to kiss him before I got in Amira's Bentley, but he mushed me and kept walking. Hanging my head in shame, I got in the passenger side. Shit like this had me feeling down, this dude was mean as hell when he didn't get his way.

Amira didn't say much until we pulled up to the house she had rented just for this weekend. She was hosting my baby shower in the back yard. Before I could get out, she grabbed my hand and stopped me. "Ru, you know you don't have to stay with him. I mean just because your having a baby you don't have to put up with that shit. You deserve better, and you don't need him for anything. You know you and the baby got me, and Remee will always be there too."

"I know, it's not that bad. I swear, he is just jealous. When Remee named the club after me, he just started feeling some kind of way. After today I'm sure he will come around." She looked unsure, and I leaned over as much as I could with my big belly in the way to hug her. "I love you bestie, now come on I'm starving and need to get some of this good food you promised would be here." She grinned and got out so we could head back. I felt the tears start to form in my eyes when I saw the yard. I didn't even know you could do no shit like this outside, but it was so pretty. Now I knew why they wanted to do the event in the evening. I was in awe as I looked at the hundreds of gold lanterns that filled the back yard. Neat rows of balloons with twinkling lights inside bordered the space, and even the pool was filled with lanterns, and dozens of pink and white roses floated in their midst.

At least twenty tables were scattered at intervals across the yard and had me wondering who the hell they had invited. Each one with a stark white tablecloth and completed with mini balloon arches. In the middle of each arch was either a blinged-out tiara or baby bottle's filled with fake diamonds that acted as a centerpiece. On each side of where the guests would sit, was a candy table and a cake table. Both of them had used balloons to turn the tables into princess carriages. And the cake, I had never seen anything like it. It was three tiers, the first tier was pink with an antique gold crown on top. The middle tier was cream with gold and pink writing that said *Welcome Baby A'Laya*. And the bottom tier sat on an antique gold platter. It was pink with a diamond design in it and gold beads in the creases. To top it off, two pink baby shoes made with fondant and gold accents sat leaned against the cake.

The huge balloon castle stole the show, inside what was supposed to be the door was a custom backdrop with the words Princess A'Laya in gold script. I noticed the photographer ready and waiting for guests to take their pictures. Just when I thought that was all, I spotted the blinged out his and hers throne at the end of the yard with a pink carpet leading the way. I groaned when I saw all the gifts piled up next to the chairs. So many boxes that my tiny apartment had no room for.

"What's up baby mama," Remee said, creeping up behind me and pulling me back against him. His hand went to my belly, and he left it there in a possessive manner. I honestly didn't even know any men would be here, but it explained the bar in the corner where Cahir was currently opening a bottle of Ace of Spades. I wished I could have a drink right now because being in Remee's presence had me stressed the fuck out.

"Remee, what are you doing?" I asked in an exasperated tone.

"The fuck you mean?" he responded as he led me to one of the tables. As soon as I sat down Amira, her mom and some of their cousins joined me. A'Remee used that moment to slip away and start greeting guests. I knew I was playing with fire, with him being here acting the part of my child's father. If this got back to Jordan, I had to prepare for a fight. I didn't know how to control Remee. And I didn't want to put out bad energy on a day that was supposed to be filled with joy, so I was going to just let things flow.

The baby shower was better than I could have imagined. Everyone participated in the games, even the guys. It was funny as hell watching some of their antics. The food wasn't like any other baby shower food I ever had. Waiters literally took your order from the customized menus. The choices ranged from different cuts of steak to lobster and shrimp. By the time I finished my piece of cake, I was ready to fall asleep at the table. "Aht aht, it's time for gifts," Amira shouted in excitement. When I saw even more presents being carried outside, I straight went to grilling the whole McKenzie family as I mentally pictured all this shit I had to bring home.

Remee came over to help me up, and I appreciated it because I was so stuffed, I could barely move. As he led me to the thrones, I realized one was for him. Not for the first time today, I noted how his outfit coordinated with mine. He was rocking a white blazer with a pink button-up shirt, white Versace jeans and white Versace sneakers. He really had shit planned out. Sitting next to me, he grabbed my hand and smiled while a ton of people took pictures and went on live. So now this shit was all over social media. Basically, after today Jordon was beating my ass. I gave Remee a look as I quickly moved my hand from his.

I opened gifts for over two hours, even with the help of Remee and Amira. I had shit that I didn't even know existed for a baby. Like a mini blender to make baby food and a spa bathtub. This shit really had jets in it. I thanked all of my guests and got up, ready to take my tired body home and get some sleep.

"Ok, before everyone leaves, Rumor has one more gift," Amira announced. "If everyone can, please follow me to the front." My stomach was in knots trying to figure out what the hell kind of gift I had that couldn't fit in the backyard. I trailed all of the guests to the front and felt my mouth drop at the new Lexus truck in the driveway with a huge bow on it. I instantly looked at Remee because I knew this shit was all him. "Here ma, it's a push gift," he said as he handed me the keys.

Amira immediately thanked the guests for coming again and got everyone on their way. I felt like she was trying to give me and Remee some privacy. "Thank you," I said as I gave him a hug. I went to kiss his cheek, but at the last minute, he turned his head, so his lips captured mine. He made sure to palm my ass and bring me as close as he could with this big ass belly in between us. He deepened the kiss, causing my pussy to throb. I had been horny as fuck lately, but me and Jordan hadn't been having sex much because we couldn't get along.

"I can't believe he bought her that expensive ass truck. Shit, I heard it wasn't even his baby." Someone commented as they walked past us. I tore my lips from his and tried to step out of his arms. Hearing that shit had brought me down from my happy place. What was I even doing with Remee right now? I was ashamed of having a baby with a busta ass nigga, and at the same time, I was ashamed of damn near cheating on him with my ex on the front lawn. Now I had Remee out here looking like a sucka for doing all this extra shit for a baby that wasn't his. My emotions were all fucked up, and I was suddenly sadder than I had been my whole pregnancy.

"Rumor fuck them, you bout to let that shit bother you? People always going to talk, shit I don't care. Let em. You and I know what it is." I just shook my head to keep from crying. I knew if I tried to talk, I wasn't going to be able to without breaking down.

I took a few small breaths and tried to calm down. Out of nowhere, I was having a damn anxiety attack on top of everything else. I hated that the night was ending this way. Remee and his family had gone all out for me. Shit, my own mother and sister would have never did all of this. I hadn't even heard from them since she put me out, pregnant with nowhere to go. I felt dizzy, and I just knew I was about to end up passed out. It only took a few minutes before my tiny breaths to turn into heaves. "Yo Rumor, what's wrong wit you ma?" Remee's concerned voice broke through the fog that my mind was turning into.

I couldn't answer because I was focusing on breathing. "Come and sit her down so I can give her some water," Amira instructed. As soon as I sat down and put my head down as far as I could, I started to feel a little better.

"Is it the baby?" he asked, his voice laced with concern. I sipped the water Amira handed me and prayed this shit was under control.

"No, she is having an anxiety attack. She started getting them after she, well, you know." She didn't finish because we all knew it was after I was damn near beaten to death. I knew he was adding this onto the guilt he already carried around. I could feel it by the way his body tensed up even more.

"I'm ok. They come and go. A lot of people get them. Sometimes it happens when I'm overly tired, and it has truly been a long day. I need to get home and crawl in my bed. I plan to sleep in tomorrow." I remembered the hundreds of gifts in the yard and felt even more tired. "Can you guys put the gifts in the house until tomorrow? I don't even know where I will be putting them in my place."

"Rumor, just stay the night. I got the place for the weekend, and there are plenty of empty bedrooms. You don't need to be driving like this. What if you fall asleep at the wheel? Plus, you already have extra clothes." Amira was right, I didn't want to take chances that could cost my baby her life.

"Ok," I reluctantly agreed as I took out my phone to call Jordan and let him know. It rang once and went to voice mail, so I just sent him a text. I wasn't about to chase this nigga.

"I will help her," Remee said, and I swear his mother smirked as we walked into the house. He grabbed my duffel bag from the couch and led me to a bedroom at the end of the hall. It was the only bedroom downstairs, and I realized it was the master. The room was huge, with a view of the pool through the sliding glass doors. The backyard was pretty much cleaned up already, the party planners have taken everything down, hauling it away. I saw Sire and a few of their workers picking up the last of the gifts to bring inside.

Remee helped me out of my dress so I could go and take a shower. It seemed like it took forever for me to scrub my body and brush my teeth, but finally, I was done. I walked into the room in only a towel thinking I would be alone, but instead Remee was there. He only had on some Polo boxers as he sat on the edge of the bed. I could tell he had showered in another bathroom because his chest still had droplets of water. I admired his tattoos, my eyes lingering on my favorite one. My name on his chest, right over his heart. I kind of thought he would have had it removed or something. Maybe he just didn't have time.

"Yo come here Ru," he said. I clenched the towel as I walked over and stood in between his legs. "What the fuck you all tensed up for? I know what you need." He slowly undid the soft material from around my body, and I felt the towel fall to the ground. Gently he sucked on my swollen nipples, first the left then the right before starting over again. I could see my juices leaking down my leg as I let out the moans I couldn't hold back anymore. I was clenching my legs together because he had me fucked up.

"Naw let me see that pretty pussy," he coaxed as he turned me around and laid me on the bed. Being on my back was uncomfortable, so I laid on my side. My legs automatically parted like they had a mind of their own. Fucking traitors, my whole body was on some rebellious, reckless behavior type shit. My mind was saying hell naw, you shouldn't be doing this. By the time I was done arguing with myself Remee had kissed his way up my legs, and I could feel his tongue brushing my clit. He ate my pussy so good I knew Amira heard me screaming. When I finally came the third time it was so intense, I prayed I didn't hurt my baby.

I never even put on clothes, just curled up on the bed, my head on his chest and fell asleep. I woke up to the sun shining through the blinds and my phone ringing. Seeing Jordan's name, I answered praying Remee ass stayed asleep. "Hello," I said making sure he could hear the sleepiness in my voice.

"Come let me in, talking about you staying the night and shit. I'm trying to see what the fuck your sneaky ass in here doing." I jumped up so fast I damn near fell on the floor. Moving as fast as I could, I threw on my panties, t-shirt and tights. Shoving all the rest of my stuff into my bag, I crept out of the bedroom and upstairs to an empty room.

"As always you showing the fuck out. Hold on I'm about to come and let you in." I hung up so I could go and warn Amira what the fuck was going on. "Mira, wake up. Girl Jordan is outside looking for me and Remee is downstairs in the bed asleep. What the fuck am I going to do?" She rolled over and put her arm over her eyes, then she let what I said sink in. She hopped up.

"Ok, well go let him in and I will try and catch Remee if he wakes up and keep him in the room." We both walked down the stairs, and I opened the door. He barged in ready to go off, but Amira stopped him. "Hey Jordan, can you keep it down some if you guys are going to talk in here. My mother is still asleep, and she hasn't been feeling well." She gave him a fake smile and a wave before going towards the back bedroom. My heart was thumping in my chest so fucking loud I could barely hear shit he said.

He was scowling at the living room filled with gifts. I swear he was a fucking hater. "Get ya shit and let's go. You coming home with me, I never told ya stupid ass to stay the night out anyway." I wanted to protest, and if it wasn't for the fact that Remee was in the house, I would have. Deciding to leave my duffel bag that was upstairs, I grabbed my Birkin and walked right out the front door. Just to show some kind of control this nigga called himself grabbing my arm.

I sent Amira a text letting her know I had to leave and to not forget my bag when she had the gifts dropped off. Jordan mumbled the whole ride to my apartment, but I didn't respond. It wasn't even worth my energy at this point. As soon as we got inside, I went right to the couch and curled up in my throw blanket. I was in desperate need of more sleep. He still wasn't done bitching about any and everything that had to do with my baby shower, and I was sick of it.

"Jordan, why are you so worried about it? You mad I got gifts? That our daughter was blessed enough to have a nice baby shower in her honor? You act like you paid for the shit! Or for anything. Why don't you shut the fuck up for real, because I'm sick of you whining?" I meant that shit from the bottom of my fucking heart too.

"Oh, you feel like you don't need a nigga, right? My little money not good enough for you and shit! I guess because I don't buy you Lexus trucks and cash out on you I don't fucking matter." I felt my heart sink when he said that. I guess he heard about the gift Remee gave me. I stood up, ready to go and get in my bed. I needed to get some rest because all of the stress in my life was getting to me. "Hell naw, you walking away from me when I'm talking to you?" Jordan snatched my arm, causing me to slam into him.

"Nigga get your hands the fuck off of me," I screamed out as

I hit him a few times in the face. Before I knew it, he had hit my stomach while trying to catch my hands. I felt a sharp pain that brought me to my knees and filled my heart with dread.

"Fuck, why was you hitting me and shit. Now look what the fuck happened." He lectured me as he walked me to the bed and helped me lay down. I was trying to remain calm, my baby was still moving around, kicking me, and I didn't feel another pain. "Rumor, just call me when the baby is coming because fucking with a bitch like you will have me facing twenty-five to life. I'm done wit ya ass." I felt hurt he was dropping me after he never even treated me good. But I knew I was wrong, for some reason I was always in the mix with Remee. Running back to that nigga even if it was just for one night. He was like a crack addiction. As soon as I heard my door close, I pulled the comforter over my head and went to sleep. Maybe when I woke up shit would be better.

I WOKE up to a pitch-black room and realized I slept all fucking day. My bladder was full and the baby kicking the shit out of me didn't help. As soon as I stood up, I felt warm liquid rush down my legs and onto the floor. I still felt like I had to pee, so I knew my water broke. And with it came pain that I wouldn't wish on anybody. I called Jordan a few times, but he sent me to voice-mail. Sending him a text, I told him I was in labor. He. Read the message but never responded. *Fuck*. I called an ambulance instead because I didn't think I could drive myself anywhere. I let Amira and Miss Layla know I was going to have the baby as I got my stuff together. She was coming a month early, and I knew it was because her retarded ass father hit my belly.

By the time the paramedics came, I had washed up, put on a clean pajama set and packed my hospital bag. They wheeled me out on a stretcher and raced me to Strong Hospital. "I'm not due until June twenty-ninth," I told them in a shaky voice.

"Ok ma'am, it will be all right. We just need you to calm down and let us make sure you have a safe delivery," the man instructed as he put an oxygen mask over my face. By the time we made it to the hospital, I was starting to feel scared. I didn't want to do this all alone, and it was clear that Jordan wasn't coming. Just like he hadn't come through for anything else since I had gotten pregnant.

As soon as I was inside, they took me to a room. I was handed a bunch of papers to sign and asked a lot of questions that I could barely focus on since the contractions were kicking my ass. I wanted to call Remee, I needed him, but he wasn't the father. I was pretty sure he wouldn't even want to be here. "Ma'am is there anyone we can call to come and be with you," the doctor asked, a look of pity on her face.

Before I could answer the door opened, and Amira was there with Miss Layla. I was so relieved I started to cry. "Don't cry sweetie, you and the baby will be alright," Miss Layla said as she came and held my hand. "I pray for this baby every night, and I know God will not take away my first granddaughter. So, you are not allowed to stress."

"The fuck she stressing for," Remee said from the doorway. A part of me wanted him to stay away, it was less complicated. But another part of me was happy as fuck he came. For the first time since I went into labor, I finally felt like everything was going to be ok.

"Perfect timing dad, we are going to get her ready to push. She is dilated to ten and fully effaced. I wanted to ask was there time for drugs, but the way the doctor snapped on her blue gloves let me know I was probably too late. "Ok on three you are going to push," she counted down, and I pushed. I felt like I was about to fall out. I swear she had me pushing for thirty damn minutes. I was squeezing Rem's hand so hard I thought I broke one of his fingers. But finally, I felt a release of pressure and heard my baby girl crying. Remee cut the cord, and I swore this nigga was crying.

They cleaned my baby up, and she screamed the whole time. I wondered would she be going to the NICU. I had no idea how small she was compared to what she should have been. "Well mom and dad, she is a bit early, and a little on the small side but fully developed. She weighs five pounds, nine ounces." As soon as she placed my daughter in my arms, I felt like the world stopped. She was beautiful, with a head full of dark silky hair and my hazel eyes. She didn't have one thing from her father, and I was grateful for that. I wanted no reminders of that mistake.

I WOKE up the next morning sore as fuck. I had sent Miss Layla and Amira home in the early hours of the morning so they could get some rest. I was sure Sire and Cahir would be back with them later on. I tried to get Remee to leave, but he ended up falling asleep in the chair next to my bed. He was still sitting there now except he wasn't sleeping. He had A'Laya on his bare chest asleep. She was so small he only needed one hand to hold her whole body in place. I could tell by the way he was looking he was deep in thought. Once he realized I was awake, his gaze shifted to mine.

"Ru, I want to talk to you about some real shit ma." I sat up as best I could in the tiny hospital bed and gave him my attention. I hoped he wasn't about to bring up the birth certificate shit again. We had argued about it last night after everyone left. He wanted to sign his name as Laya's father, but I refused to let him. It wasn't fair to her, him or Jordan. She had a father who may someday want to be in her life. And she needed to know who he was. Plus, Remee shouldn't be taking on responsibility for someone else's child. He was mad as fuck, but I held my ground.

"I need you to know that even though she won't have my last name, for now, I meant every word I said. This is my daughter. I am going to be there for everything, first word, first step, the first day of school. Anything she needs I got that, anything you need I got that. I love you the same as I always have. I never came close to loving any other woman the way I feel about you Ru. I need you to know that shit is real. But I'm going to be real wit you. I can't be your man right now, maybe not ever. I don't want to break your heart again or cause harm to come your way. And I can't promise you that I won't be out here with one of these bitches. This lifestyle comes with a lot of shit, and I just ain't learned to grow above it yet."

"Ok," I said sniveling a little. I had never thought about taking him back. But just knowing he wasn't able to commit to me hurt. Even though I appreciated his honesty.

"You going home to the projects with my daughter is dead as fuck. I hope you knew that but if you didn't," he trailed off and shrugged. "I bought ya'll a condo near my mom's spot. It has three bedrooms, a family room, laundry room and a garage. The deed is in your name, I set up a trust for A'Laya, and ten percent of my profits from the club go directly into it every month. Another twenty percent goes into your bank account for bills, clothes whatever."

"If you don't have enough money for something, ya'll call me. I cut Amira's spoiled ass off my Amex account so you will be getting the extra card for emergencies or whatever. Don't feel sad for her, she got her own bread and still live home with mom. And we both know she spending Sire and Cahir money." I smiled through my tears because Amira stayed running through all they pockets.

I wanted so bad to turn down everything he was giving me. But I knew it came from his heart. Remee had been taking care of me since I was twelve years old. When he ain't have shit, he still made sure I was good. It seemed like it was all he knew. I was determined to work, even if it was a minimum wage job, so I could make some kind of way for myself.

"You been rocking wit me since I ain't have shit, and you always got a nigga's heart. There ain't nothing you can's ask me for, nothing I won't give you just say the word. I don't want you to think a nigga don't know that money don't mean shit. I will be there, my presence will show you how much I really fucking love you. The fact I would give my life for your's should speak for itself. And someday Rumor, when I'm ready to act right, I will make you my wife.

10

SIRE

THREE YEARS LATER

I SIGHED as I walked in the house to see all the lights on. Tayari's toys were all over the floor surrounding her tiny body as the TV babysat her. I checked the time and saw it was a little after four in the morning. "Hey daddies' girl what are you still doing awake?" I asked as I tried to navigate the maze of dolls, Legos and bright colored plastic balls.

"Daddy, I wet," she said, standing up and giving me a sad smile. I noticed she was still in her clothes from earlier in the day. So, her lazy ass mother hadn't even given her a bath or put on her PJ's. I was beating Shay's ass as soon as I settled my daughter. I swear having a baby with this rat was one of the worst things I could have done. Making her my woman was the other. I gave my baby a bath, put her on some fresh pajamas and tucked her in her toddler bed. She was asleep before I could even turn on the night light.

I walked down the hall to the bedroom me and her mother shared when I was here. There were a lot of reasons I still kept my own spot. And me not murdering this bitch was one of them.

Shay was curled up in the ten thousand count sheets, sleeping without a care in the world, like she didn't even realize our kid was home. I snatched her up by the back of her neck and shook her out of her sleep. "The fuck you in here sleeping for and Tayari is downstairs, alone, pissy and watching TV in the middle of the night. You know how much shit a two-year-old can get into when no one is watching?" Luckily my daughter was smart as fuck for being two and rarely touched things she shouldn't.

"Nigga fuck you, I was tired and her ass wouldn't settle down. I'm not waiting on no kid to go to sleep. Maybe if you would have brought your ass in here at a reasonable time you could have helped." She flung herself back down on the bed and tried to look sexy like I wasn't just roughing her up. Or we were not in the middle of discussing why my daughter wasn't being taken care of. Lately shit between Shay and me had been worse than ever. And I'm noticing the more we argue, the worse she treated my daughter.

I leaned onto the bed and put my hand around her neck. "Bitch, listen to me and listen good. When it comes down to my daughter and anyone, my daughter always comes first. If you don't start taking care of her the way a mother should, I mean asap I'm killing ya ass. I can do this shit by myself or hire a fucking nanny to do a better job than you. If I ever come into the house and see my shorty the way she was tonight, I'm killing you. This shit ain't a game, I ain't ya little goofy, hoe ass friends. You got two jobs around here. Take care of Tayari and have the pussy ready when I want it. In exchange you living ya best life." I added a little pressure to her throat and watched the panicked look cross her face. Finally, I let go and dropped her to the bed. Standing up, I had the desire to go and wash my hands before I left.

"You're not staying," she sniffled as I came out of the bathroom and headed to the bedroom door.

Declining to answer, I ignored her tears and walked out the door.

"Son, this shit is about to hit right now," my boy Jax said as we walked through the door of the Burger King. "I swear I be in this motherfucker every day eating this shit."

"That's why yo ass fat as fuck now," Grip said mugging Jax and causing us all to laugh. I mean the shit wasn't a lie, Jax was one of those dudes that dressed smooth as fuck to try and hide the fact he was carrying a big ass belly in front of him. If he was a female I would have thought he was about to give birth. He used to be tall and skinny when he was broke, but that money had his ass eating good.

"Fuck you nigga, you can suck my fat dick," Jax responded as he grilled Grip. Grip was my right hand, so I wasn't worried about this shit going too far, at least not in public. He was smart and made calculated moves, shit he had to be in order to be at the top of my organization. But I knew one of these days he was going to leave Jax stinking somewhere. He hated that nigga, and they were always getting into it.

It was rare that I kicked it with the crew, but these days it was better than being home. I had been smoking all day, and suddenly a Whopper felt like the best thing in the world. "Yo why that bitch ain't serving me," Jax said to the annoyed looking white man who was trying to take his order. He motioned to someone on the other side of the dining room.

"Sir, she is on her break. Is there anything I can get for you today?"

Instead of responding, Jax walked in the direction of a woman sitting at a table with her back to us. I groaned internally; this dude had a bad history with the females. They either wanted him for his money or didn't want him at all. And let's just say he didn't take rejection well. "Here this dumb nigga go, he can't even get some food without being on some fuck boy shit," Grip said as we stood there waiting to see what was going to happen next.

He ran his hand over the girl's hair that was in two French braids, causing her to jump up. "Nigga, why are you touching me," she hissed. Her voice was filled with venom as she continued. "I keep telling you I'm not interested in fucking with you. No, I don't want to be yo girlfriend, side chick, or whatever else you have in mind, now please leave me alone."

"Bitch, I know you need a dude like me in your life. I can get you up out of this shit. You just need to stay home and be ready for daddy. Stop acting like you don't need the money. Shit, your sister had no problem taking this dick for a few bills, so you don't have to pretend that you not down for the cause."

Shorty jumped up and ran across the table to cover a little girls' ears. Hell, I didn't even notice little mama sitting there. But I knew Jax did. For some reason, that shit had me heated. Probably because I had a little girl at home. I walked closer to them so I could cut this encounter short. "What is wrong with you? You see me sitting here with my daughter, right?" I noticed the coloring books and crayons spread across the table in front of them. Shorty was spending time with her kid any way she could, and I respected that.

"I don't give a fuck about your kid being here Bella. This a business, not a fucking daycare. Her little ass not even supposed to be in this mother fucker." Hearing him say Bella caused my focus to shift from the little girl to the mom. It couldn't be her, but it was. Shorty was still rocking the charm bracelet I had bought her for her birthday years ago. Even in her work clothes, I could tell her body was the truth, and she was still pretty as fuck. Her face had a more mature look, but I could tell it was her. I would never forget Arabella, she did something to a nigga's heart. Something no other women had been able to do after all this time.

I had low key looked for her the past three years. I still remember the last time I saw her, how pretty she was, how stressed she looked. I worried about her and the child she was carrying. I wondered was she mine. But I was sure Bella would have reached out to me by now if she was. I searched her tiny face seeing if she had any of my features and I didn't see any. She looked just like her mother. Same caramel skin tone, almond shaped eyes and small ears. The only difference was the small dusting of freckles across her nose.

"Bells," I said, calling out to her. She looked up at me and stopped talking mid-sentence. Her hands fell away from her daughter's head, and she looked shocked.

"Sire," she said in disbelief. Her face lit up with joy, then her expression became closed off. "Jael, take your coloring book and go sit at the table over there for mommy," she directed her daughter. Once the little girl was settled and cheerfully coloring again, she turned her attention back to me. "It's nice to see you, Sire. I hope you have been good."

"Bitch, the fuck you talking to him for? He doesn't want you, the fuck a boss look like fucking wit a rat who works at BK." Jax moved closer to her, and I was mad as fuck.

"So, I have been told a few times before," Bella commented as she turned to walk away from both of us. That shit hit a nigga in the chest. I remembered when her sister told her I wouldn't be interested in her. But I was then and I still was now. I didn't even remember I had a women at home. I just needed to get to Bella.

"Nigga don't say shit else to her," I barked seeing Jax open his thick ass mouth ready to respond. "Any time you see her, don't say a fucking word to her. That right there is all me, she been all me." Everyone with me looked confused as fuck, but the best part of being a boss was I didn't have to answer to any fucking body. "Ya'll move around," I demanded, and everyone went back to order their food. "You good ma," I asked as I went to stand in front of her. She smelled like vanilla her scent had my dick hard. I tried to focus on what she was saying instead of thoughts of how good her pussy was.

"Yes, I'm good. Thanks, Sire, I appreciate you coming to my rescue once again." She offered a slight smile before turning her back on me. Shorty was straight dismissing me and shit. It was amusing because most days I couldn't get the hoes to leave me alone, but here she was damn near running away from me. It was a lot I had to say to Arabella, starting with who the fuck was the father of her little girl. Even though I had figured out I wasn't the father I wanted to be sure. The thought of her having a baby with someone else had me feeling sick as fuck. For his sake, I hoped they weren't still together because I was taking Bella from him.

"Yo give me your number," I said, pulling out my phone and walking up behind her.

"Sire, I don't think that's a good idea," she said her gaze shifting towards Jax. "It was nice seeing you, but I have to get back to work." I nodded, letting her get by. This wasn't the last she would be seeing of me.

I had Grip drop me off at my truck since I rode with him. "Yo who the fuck is shorty? Looks like she got ya ass sprung." He asked as he parked behind my Porsche Cayenne.

"No bitch ever had me sprung and don't fucking worry about who she is."

"Well shit, she looks like she got that pussy that will fuck up a nigga's head. I'm going to try and find out for myself. I'm ready to get sprung off her good shit." He laughed when I pulled my gun out and set it on my lap. "Just like I thought, next time tell the truth nigga before I take your fucking girl for real. But seriously, you gonna have bigger problems than my fine ass. Shay is going to eat that sweet little girl up and spit her out. If you really care about her, the best thing you can do is stay away from her. Your life isn't for the faint of heart."

Sitting back, I knew he was right. I had beef with niggas I didn't even know I had beef with in these streets because everyone wanted to be at the top. My baby mother was a true hood rat who loved to keep up drama. And I spent most of my time fucking random hoes, arguing with Shay or moving cocaine around the country. But I couldn't walk away from Arabella, leaving her alone just wasn't an option. She was the one thing I had desired over the past few years that I couldn't have. The only thing that money couldn't give me. As selfish as it was, I wanted Bella, and I was going to have her.

"I can see you made up your mind. I hope that shit works out for you. One of these days, I look forward to hearing all about how you know shorty. But for now, get the fuck out of my truck, I got some shorty at the hotel waiting on me to bust down her throat." I dapped up Grip before getting out of his shit. We had been friends since we were little niggas and, in a world, filled with snakes I appreciated having someone solid to watch my back.

I drove straight back to the Burger King and double-parked out front. I paid the manager five hundred dollars to tell me what time Bella's shift ended. I patiently waited another hour before getting out and heading inside. I looked around and didn't see her or her daughter, and I wondered was someone trying to play me. Homie wasn't just going to run back my money he was paying with his life.

"Yo homie, where the fuck Bella at?" I asked the nigga working behind the counter.

"She in the back somewhere. But you wasting your time with that one. Her stuck up ass act like she too good to fuck anybody. Like her pussy made of gold or some shit." He rolled his eyes like a bitch. Reaching behind the counter, I grabbed him by the front of his uniform and bust his ass upside the head.

"So, she stuck up because she not ok with fucking every nigga that walk through the door? When it comes to Bella and who she fucking going forward mind ya business." That was why these dudes ended up with a bunch of kids with hoes that can barely spell their names and shit. They be out here worried about the wrong shit. I let his shifty-eyed ass go, and he hit his jaw on the counter as he went down. His mouth filled with blood as he stood up and ran to the back. Customers were looking at me crazy and shit, but no one said anything. I was happy the general public was making safe decisions tonight.

"Ok Jael, let's go out our Uber will be here soon," she said to her daughter who she was holding in her arms as she walked from the back. The little girl looked tired the way she had her head laid on Bella's shoulder. Once Bella saw me standing there, she made a face. "Can I help you with something Sire?"

"Damn Bella, you treating me real fucked up right now. I'm about to just be straight wit you, I miss you ma. I'm just trying to be a part of your life again."

She sighed and shifted the little girl to the other side of her hip. I could tell she was getting heavy. "Sire, I missed you too, but as you can see, my life isn't about me anymore. I have priorities, and I just am not in a place to entertain any man and his bullshit. Now I really have to go because my ride will be here soon." She reached out her hand to gently touch mine for a second and then she was headed for the door.

Following behind her, I knew she wasn't getting in no fucking Uber unless she wanted me to put a hot one in the driver. "Bella at least let me take you home," I said. Her daughter lifted her head up and smiled at me. "Hey pretty girl," I said, making her giggle.

"I'm not pretty girl, I'm Jael," she responded.

"Ok Jael, I'm Sire. It's nice to meet you." She smiled again. Bella's phone dinged interrupting our conversation. She huffed as she looked at her Uber app. It showed the driver cancelled, and they were finding her a new ride.

"Bells, come on I swear I ain't on no funny shit. Just let me take ya'll home. It's getting late, and shorty looks tired as fuck."

"Just a ride Sire, nothing else. And you can drop me off down the street from my house. I don't need you knowing where I live." She sassed.

Opening the doors for her and Jael I waited until they were settled in before heading to the driver's side. "Arabella, I wish I would leave you in the middle of the road wit baby girl at night.

Or at any fucking time. You used to busta ass niggas for real. Anyway, I don't need to drop you off to find out where you live. I would have figured that shit out anyway."

"Let me guess, you're the reason why my manager had a sudden windfall, and my coworker came in the back bleeding all over the place. Sire, you wild as fuck, I see ain't nothing about you changed."

❦ II ❦

ARABELLA

SIRE JUST CHUCKLED and kept driving while I gave him directions to my place. Luckily I lived in a complex so he wouldn't know which apartment exactly I stayed in. "So, talk to me Arabella? What has been going on all these years that you have been out of my life?"

"Well, I'm a mom, I work at Burger King and I attend Culinary school. That's about it, my favorite hang out spot these days is Chuck E Cheese," I said giggling.

"Damn you gonna have to take me to your hang out spot so I can have fun too." I just shook my head at him. The whole drive we caught up on basic shit. Being around Sire was a whole vibe, it was like we just clicked with no effort. If anything, that should have scared me the most about him, because I wasn't beat for nothing serious with any man. I had already learned my lesson on that.

"Ok Sire you can pull up to the building right here and let me out. It really was nice seeing you." I unbuckled waiting on him to stop, instead of pulling up where I told him he parked in a guest spot and hopped out. I watched as he came around to open my door. Sire was still fine as fuck, I mean he was cute when I first met him, but he was on some grown ass man shit now. His body looked cut the fuck up through his V-neck Armani tee. He still wore his hair with those low-cut curls, except now he had a little beard going on. I blushed thinking about the way I used to grab his curls when he would eat my pussy.

"What the fuck you over here thinking about," he said, giving me a knowing look.

"Nothing, nosey. Now please move out of my way so I can grab Jael and get inside. I told you to pull up close to the door." I stepped down from his truck only for him to be there, crowding my space. I tried to push past, but his body was like a rock.

"Bella, I tried to find you," he said, causing me to look up. "After the day at the block party. I looked for you, I even broke in your parent's spot, but it looked like you all had moved. I never forgot about you." He leaned down and kissed me, causing my body to stiffen. I began struggling to breathe, and at this point, I just felt like I had to get away from him, and the situation. "Bella, what's wrong ma, talk to me." He sounded concerned, and I felt embarrassed that something as little as a kiss caused me to have a damn panic attack. I really had no control over them, and they just came randomly.

I dropped my head as I caught my breath. I told myself over and over again that it was just Sire. Not Alex or anyone else who has caused me pain. "Sorry Sire, like I said I'm not the same girl you knew. I really need to get inside." I grabbed my purse and Jae's bag from inside the car and hurried to open the back door. Jael was still sound asleep, and I dreaded the idea of carrying her up the stairs. "I got her," Sire said as he carefully unbuckled her and picked her up. "I was walking you to the door anyway." My emotions were all over the place, so I just walked to my apartment with no argument.

Unlocking the door, I let Sire walk in first, and I followed. I could see him looking around my spot being nosey as fuck again. "You can set her down on the couch." I watched as he gently laid her down and then took her shoes off. He was good with kids, and I wondered if he had any. Imagining him having kids for some reason had me feeling some kind of way. I watched as Sire walked into my kitchen and stood in front of my fridge for a few minutes. I hoped getting him to leave wasn't going to be a big ass headache. This was why I didn't want him to come up, to begin with. I was still standing by the door when he headed towards me.

"Aight ma, I'm going to get out of your way. My number is on the fridge since you refuse to give me yours. Bella, just know whatever you went through doesn't matter to me. A nigga doesn't give up easy so just remember that. Can I kiss you before I leave?" I thought I would feel relief hearing he was leaving, but for some reason, I was feeling the opposite. The girl who fell in love with Sire years ago was inside of me crying out for him to stay, for him to protect me from my demons. Both the ones seen and unseen. He opened the door not asking about a kiss again.

"Sire," I called out softly. "One kiss." Sire turned and pulled me closer to him, even though my heart was racing the panic from earlier was gone. I buried my face in his chest for a second and smelled his cologne. I didn't know the scent, but it was the same as he wore when I knew him. Being this close to him again was like the dreams I had. I never got over Sire, even after all I went through with Alex, then with Derrick, Sire was always there in my heart. His hand slid under my chin and lifted my head up, so I was looking in his eyes. I couldn't read them, but instead of the normal honey color, they turned darker. Almost like an amber. His lips touched mine, and I coached myself to relax, except I didn't have to. I got lost in his kiss, his soft lips covering mine had my pussy jumping, and I knew I for sure had to stay away from Sire McKenzie.

He stopped the kiss and stepped back. "You be good Bells, I will see you soon."

"Goodbye, Sire," I said low as I closed the front door behind him.

SIRE DIDN'T COME AROUND for at least two weeks after the night he kissed me. I went to work every day with thoughts of him on my mind. Somewhat relieved when he didn't show up and somewhat sad. I knew playing with him was playing with fire, and I had no time to get burned. Just when I thought Sire had forgotten about me, his ass damn near became a stalker. The whole month of June he had been at my job almost every night. He refused to let me uber or take a bus home no matter how I fought him on the issue. Some days I would be working and just look out into the dining room to see him sitting there, watching me, and I guess today was no different. I was determined not to let Sire break me down. Even if I wasn't emotionally fucked up, I would have steered clear of him. I knew he was a lady's man, and that wasn't something I was interested in.

Today he had on a white and gold Polo shirt, jean shorts and a pair of white Jordans. When he walked in, he nodded to my manager who gave him some slick ass smile. Probably hoping to get paid for more info on me. I noticed the gift bags with him, and I was confused because it wasn't my birthday. The last hour of my shift dragged by because I was anxious to find out what the fuck Sire was up to. Finally, I was able to clock out, and I swear I almost ran from behind the counter. "Sire, what the fuck you buying me gifts for?" I snapped glaring at him.

"Bella, I ain't buy you a damn thing. This shit ain't for you. And why you barking on a nigga like you wasn't excited by the thought of a gift from your man." All I could do was giggle because I was like a kid waiting on some candy when I thought about the gifts. I felt stupid now that I had assumed the shit was for me. "Don't look sad baby girl, daddy got a gift for you right here." He looked down, and I could see how hard his dick was through his shorts. I should have been mad, but I swear Sire kept my ass amused when he came around so instead, I almost fell out laughing. "Damn ma, I didn't remember him being that funny when I had your legs pinned next to your ears, and you were screaming my name," he said low enough so only I could hear. I turned beat red remembering the moment he was talking about.

"Mommy," Jael called as she skipped inside of the Burger King, her little sparkly pink backpack bouncing with her. I waved at her bus driver before opening my arms so she could run into them. This was the best part of my day. "Hi mister Sire," she said and ran to give him a hug too. Somehow over the past month, she had become attached to Sire even though she would only see him during the rides home, he insisted on giving me.

"Hey Jael, guess what? I have some gifts for you." My daughter's tiny mouth formed into an O when he sat the gift bags in front of her. I hid my smile, happy to know he wasn't buying shit for some other girl. I hated to admit it, but Sire was breaking me down more and more every day.

"Ooooh thank you sooo much Sire," Jael said as she dragged the bags over to a table and set down. I guess she couldn't wait until we got home, or until I gave my approval. I watched her squeal as she pulled a doll out of the first one. It looked like it came with diapers and jars of fake food and I swear if it made a mess in my house, Sire was getting his ass beat. Next were a few outfits that I knew were designer. A Frozen II Lego set that made me want to cry because I knew the pieces would be everywhere. The last bag had my baby jumping up and down so much I couldn't even see what as in her hand. Finally, my eye caught the Apple logo and had me catching an attitude.

"Sire, she cannot accept that. Really any of this, but the iPad for sure has to go back." Jael looked up at me with her lip quivering. "Jael, that is a very expensive gift, and we cannot accept it from Sire. So, mommy needs you to give that one back like a good girl." At three, my baby was not only very smart, but she was also very well behaved.

"Here you go," she said as tears filled her eyes and she handed the tablet back towards him. I hated that he put her in this position. He should have never bought her no shit that cost more than my whole paycheck.

"Arabella, don't do that ma. I bought it for her to have it. You bought to break her heart because of what? You scared to take a gift from me? This not even about you, trust." The look he shot my way gave me a chill. I didn't know if he was hurt or mad or both, but he wasn't fucking with me at the moment. Sire refused to take it back; instead, he helped Jael put everything in the bags, and they walked to his car. No one even looked back to see if I was coming. The ride to my place was silent except for Jael in the back playing with her new doll. Usually, we would be talking about everything from the weather to books. He double-parked, and I knew he wasn't even coming inside.

I climbed out and gathered all of our stuff. "Bye mister Sire and thank you again," Jael called out. She stopped long enough to hug Sire, who was leaned against the back of the truck before she raced off towards the door.

"Thank you, Sire, for making her happy." I didn't even look at him since he didn't have shit to say. Before I got far, he had grabbed my arm and pulled me over to him.

"Here, this one was for you," he said, sliding the small bag from Kays my way. "Just because I'm mad at you don't mean I ain't fucking wit you. The same thing applies like always, if you need me, call me." He kissed me on my forehead and walked away.

❦

"MOMMY, CAN I HAVE THESE," Jael asked, holding up the sparkly silver and pink Converses. I knew she wasn't going to wear them every day, but they didn't cost much, and my baby usually didn't ask for too much.

"Ok, we will get these and the Jordans. Now we have to go because the store is closing." I waited for the sales lady to ring us up, then used my bank card to pay. I didn't splurge a lot on myself, but I liked to make sure my baby was fly. After thanking the cashier, I grabbed our bags and headed for the door. As soon as I stepped foot outside, I ran into a hard body. "Sorry," I said without looking. I was making sure Jael was still behind me.

"Wow, what a pretty girl just like your mommy," a familiar voice said. His voice caused my knees to get weak and a chill to run through my body. I immediately pulled Jael closer to me and backed away. Alex stood in front of me with an evil grin on his face. "Where are you running off to with my daughter Arabella? I've been looking for you a long time now and look at God. You just appeared before me like a miracle."

"How dare you bring God in to this, you sick son of a bitch. This isn't your daughter, and don't fucking speak to her." I kept backing up with Jael clinging on to me. She could sense something was wrong and was gripping the shit out of my hand. Alex began laughing, and even though he didn't follow me, I could see it in his eyes, he was plotting on how to get to us. I didn't know what to do because now that the mall was closing, I would have to go outside, and I was sure he knew that too. Waiting outside at the bus stop would make us a sitting duck. I went to the main entrance and waited near the door but didn't go outside yet. I looked at the time, and I only had five minutes before they would start telling us to leave.

I hurried and called Sire praying he picked up, we hadn't spoken since I pissed him off the other day. He sent some texts just to check on us, but that was all. "Yo," he answered.

"Sire, can you please come and pick us up at the mall out in Greece. Please, I'm scared." He didn't ask any questions just told whoever he was with to make a turn and head this way.

"G hand me my gun from the glove compartment. Shorty, I'm on my way. And Bella don't hang up this fucking phone until I get there."

Looking through the glass doors, I saw Alex's black pick up truck outside. He was smirking at me through the open window. I started crying. I didn't want Jael to get hurt in any way by this man. I could try and fight him, but I knew he was stronger than me. I also knew he had a shotgun in the back of that truck. He always had. "Don't cry ma, I'm almost there. Remee drive faster or pull the fuck over." I almost laughed at his ignorant ass, he was rude as fuck and kept cursing at his brother who must have been driving.

"Ma'am the mall is closed, and you need to exit the premises." Some fat security guard said as he ushered everyone around me outside. "Come on ladies and gentlemen its time to go home, we are closed." I walked out as slow as I could. I stood with the small group of people waiting for the bus, praying that would deter Alex. But my prayers were not answered.

"Bella, you can make this hard or easy. But it's time for you to come home with daddy." Alex was next to me with his hand on my shoulder and a wicked grin on his face. I tried to snatch away from him, but he tightened his hold.

"Mommy," Jael called out uncertainly. Her eyes were wide with fear, and I could see the tears swimming in them.

"It's ok baby. We are about to go home, and you can have some ice-cream." I was skeptical that I was about to make it home, but I wanted to reassure my baby. I suddenly dropped my stuff and Jael's hand, then I swung on Alex. I don't think I was really doing shit, but at least I was trying. Alex let go of my shoulder, and I thought I was winning until I felt my face sting from him backhanding me.

"Bitch, go get in the fucking truck." I tasted blood in my mouth and felt defeated. My phone was on the ground, so I didn't even know if Sire was close. I made sure I let the blood pool in my mouth before I spit right in his face. His hand was around my neck faster than lightning, and I could hear my baby screaming.

I was barely conscious, and at this point, all the blood was rushing to my head. I couldn't believe all the fucking people were just standing here watching this shit play out. I bet if I was at the boujee mall in Victor, someone would have called the cops. Or at least tried to help. All of a sudden I could breathe. I took a few seconds to try and focus my eyes and get some air in my lungs. "Yo put her in the truck and stay with her," I heard Sire demand as I saw one of his boys pick Jael up and bring her to the truck. I heard scuffling as Sire started beating the hell out of Alex. I just assumed he shot people. I had no idea he could throw hands. He broke his nose, and what sounded like his jaw next. Blood was everywhere, and finally, his brother stopped him when sirens could be heard in the distance.

"Son, we gotta roll," Remee said as he stepped in. He walked over to me and tried to check me over, but Sire was there damn near shoving him out of the way. He picked me up and climbed in the back of the truck.

"Bells you good," he asked as his hands roamed my body. I guess he thought I had some broken bones. I nodded because if I started talking, I was going to just cry harder. I held my arms out for my daughter, and he held both of us close. "Yo drop me out in EV, have someone bring me the Benz," he told his brother before he focused on me again. "I'm so fucking sorry it took so long. This nigga drives slow as fuck." He literally grilled his brother from the back.

"Fuck I look like a getaway driver," he shot back at him. "My bad ma, I forgot the little one is back there."

"It's ok," I said giving him a weak smile. I only knew Remee was Sire's brother because my best friend worked in one of his clubs and loved to tell me stories about the McKenzie brothers. I think she wanted me to ask her to help me get in touch with Sire. But I had let go of that dream years ago. We made it to my house fast since I didn't live that far away from the mall.

"Aight family, I will get up wit ya'll later. Grip, hit me when you drop off the car." He carried Jael and helped me inside. I watched as he helped her put away her new sneakers played with her and even gave her ice-cream.

"Ok Jae, bath time then bed," I said, hoping she would give me a hard time tonight. I wasn't ready to have that talk with Sire about Alex, and I could tell by the way he was looking that he was waiting. I went into the bathroom to run a bubble bath and wash my baby up.

"Bella, I'm about to step out for a second ma. Where your key at?"

"On the kitchen table," I yelled down the hall. He must have found it because I heard my front door close.

By the time I was helping Jael into her Doc McStuffins PJs, her eyes were half-closed. "Mommy, is Sire coming back?" Her lower lip was poked out, and I was shocked at her even asking for Sire.

"Yes he will be back, why, do you like Sire?"

"Yes, I like Sire, he is fun Plus, he will keep the bad man away from us." The last part had me feeling like shit. I never wanted my daughter to be scared of anything, and what happened today was going to fuck with her for a long time. Besides just because Sire saved me today, didn't mean that was the end of Alex. I hated to think what could happen next time.

"She good," he asked startling me. I didn't even hear him come back in. I looked down to see her already asleep. Covering her up, I placed a kiss on her forehead and followed him into the living room.

"She was worried that you weren't coming back. Apparently, you have a new fan."

"Shit, lil mama got good taste. She recognizes real." I laughed at him, boosting himself up.

"Yea, you aight." I replied as I laid my head on the arm of the couch. It had been a long stressful ass day. He stood in front of me and crouched down, so he was looking in my face. I felt him gently lift my face and trace the bruise around my neck. It made me shudder and think how I could have easily lost my life today.

"You need to tell me what's up with that nigga for real." He sat next to me and pulled me in his arms. "Bella, it's time for you to let me in. You can't see a nigga serious about you? Shit, I almost caught a charge behind you today."

He was right, I owed him the truth. "He's Jael's father," I said looking straight ahead at the wall. I didn't want to see his face when I said that. I felt him tense and wondered what he was thinking.

"Aint that nigga ya step pops or some shit?"

"Yea, he was my mom's boyfriend. To make a long story short, he started raping my older sister once she was eighteen and planned to do the same to me. That was why I wanted you to take my virginity. I decided to let someone I wanted to be my first and not him. After you, he started raping me regularly. When I found out I was having a girl, I knew I couldn't let her go through what I went through. He made it clear even though it was his child that she would suffer the same fate me and my sister did. The day I came to see you, I was going to ask you for help but, well you were occupied. So, I ran away. I spent some time in a homeless shelter and right before I had the baby, I got into an apartment. I hadn't seen or heard from Alex or my mom since I left home until I ran into him today."

He remained quiet for a while. All I could hear was his heart beating as he held me even closer if possible. "He was the one beating on you the day I saw you outside."

"Yea," I said low. My life made me ashamed. Some days I used to ask why me, but after a while, I just felt like there must be something wrong with me, and that was why.

"What's that nigga last name?" he questioned. His voice was flat, emotionless.

I thought about not telling him, but Sire usually found a way to get any info he wanted so it would be a waste. "Smalls."

"Ease up some Bella," he said as I shifted over on the couch. He got up and went into the kitchen. I saw him take two guns from the top of the fridge. "I will be back later."

I jumped up and ran to him, grabbing his arm. "Sire, what the hell are you going to do? I don't want you doing shit because of me. Just come back inside please Sire," I begged, but he wasn't moving. His eyes looked like the fire in hell, I guess he was filled with rage. But it wasn't that serious, not over me.

"Bella move, he was dead after today anyway. But I can't sleep until I take care of this nigga. He violated something that belonged to me." He dropped a kiss on the top of my head and then he was gone.

12

CAHIR

I APPLIED a little more pressure to Deana's neck and I swore my dick almost jumped out of the condom. This bitch was a good pick, she was holding on where others had failed. I pulled out of her pussy and slid right into her asshole. The look of pain that crossed her face had me ready to bust. That was all sex was about to me, causing these bitch's pain and getting a nut. Her face was damn near purple and I wondered was I about to go to far and kill this one. Deciding to let her live to suck and fuck another day I let my hand loose and pulled my dick out of her. With all the trauma I had caused her body I would have expected to see her pussy dried up, but instead she was dripping onto her sheets. She must have came at least three times. Giving pleasure wasn't ever my focus, but more power to her if she could get off. Seeing the bite marks all over her light skin, my dick got even harder if possible. Taking off the condom and putting on a clean one, I pushed her to her knees and shoved my dick inside.

I never gave shorty a chance to catch her breath. I was fucking her mouth hard, causing her to gag and choke. As long as she didn't throw up, this shit was a win. Pulling her natural hair, I went a little further down her throat before I felt my nut.

Pulling out, I took off the condom and bust all over her face. There was no better way to start my morning than with a hoe on her knees with a face full of my babies. "Ransom, that was so go-" Shorty must have been talking to her damn self because I was already in her bathroom flushing the condoms and wiping my dick off.

"Good looking out," I called over my shoulder as I headed for the door. I went from the hoes house to the dope house. Pulling up to the warehouse, I got out of my car and went inside. I quietly watched for a few hours, not speaking to anyone. If my cousins weren't here, I had no reason to speak. These niggas were workers, not friends. Walking to the back, I noticed this nigga Fin looking sneaky. Pretending to walk off, I watched out of the corner of my eyes as he broke off a tiny piece of the crack he was bagging up and slipped it in his pocket. I strolled over, looked him in the eyes and blew his brains out. I didn't fuck with thieves. Glancing at the head of security Hans, I nodded, so he knew to come clean this fool up. I should have shot his ass too but I didn't feel like cleaning up the bodies right now.

I saw the time and realized I had to go and meet up with Sire. I left the same way I came silently. Picking up my phone, I called to see if he was home. "Yo, son you at the crib?"

"Naw, I'm kicking it wit my people. Come meet me at the BK on Lyell."

"Aight, say less." I drove across town and parked in the tow-away zone. I didn't plan to be inside long.

"What's good," I said, walking up to my cousins. Sire had some shorty in his lap, I guess she was the one Remee told me about. I never thought he would cheat on hood rat ass Shay, but shorty had him doing more than that. He was dropping bodies and all of that. I chopped it up with him and Remee for a few and collected the paperwork I came for. I was investing in a new business, and I had Remee's lawyer look it over for me. I didn't trust any one person, so my lawyer checked it, and so did his.

Feeling someone bump into me, I turned around with a

scowl. "Yo shorty watch where the fuck you going," I barked on some chick standing there with a little boy.

"I'm sorry," she said and offered a smile.

I won't even hold you, she was pretty as fuck. I'd ran through a lot of bitches but something about her appealed to me. "Nah fuck that shit, in the future be more careful. I ain't no tiny nigga, so I know yo stupid ass saw me standing here." I watched as her smile turned into a slight frown. One of her perfectly arched eyebrows raised like she was trying to figure something out.

"I said I was sorry!" She crossed her arms over her chest like she was uncomfortable. "And could you stop staring at me, I don't want your rude ass." She had to be about five foot five because I was towering over her. Even though she had a slick ass mouth, there was something about shorty that I liked. And it wasn't just the way her body looked in her skintight jeans.

"I don't want ya ugly ass. I can have any bitch out here and trust me you not my type." Well, at least a part of what I said was true. She really wasn't my type, I could only fuck wit certain types of women, and she looked too innocent to be one of em.

"You are being mean, say sorry to my mommy," the little boy she had with her said. He stepped in front of her and looked up at me wit no fear. Lil nigga was the truth. I heard Remee snicker from behind me, and I was cursing that mother fucker out later.

"Aight little man, you got that." I held my hand out for him to dap me up, but instead, he grilled me. I chuckled, these kids were wild as fuck. "Yo shorty my bad. But still, in future be more careful." She gave me the finger and turned her attention to the chick in Sire's lap who I assumed was her friend.

"Bella, I have to go I'm running late, and you know Natalie don't play that shit. They both had dinner and should be tired soon." She leaned down and kissed her son, running her hands over his curly mohawk. A little girl I didn't even see ran out from behind her and stopped in front of Sire and his shorty.

"Mommy, Sire, he has a potty mouth," she said, pointing to me and sticking out her tongue. Shit if I didn't know better, I would think she was Sire's kid the way she just snitched on me to his ass.

"I'm sorry Eternity, I shouldn't have picked up the shift today," Bella said, looking guilty as fuck. "Thank you for keeping her, now hurry and go before you get in trouble."

"Yo don't you work at my club," Remee asked his face scrunched up like he was trying to remember. I swear he needed to quit smoking, that shit was catching up to him. I acted like I wasn't paying attention, but I was listening to every word.

"Yes, Mister McKenzie, I'm a bottle girl at Remi`." Gone was the ghetto girl who was talking shit to me. She sounded professional as fuck talking to Remee.

"You good ma, I'm going to hit Natalie up and let her know not to fuck wit you." He pulled out his phone and shot off a text.

"Thank you. I appreciate it. See ya'll later she said waving to everyone in general. She gave out smiles until she came to me. Rolling her eyes, she turned and fast walked out the door.

"Nigga you have no fucking chill, like damn she bumped into you it wasn't that serious," Sire said. I didn't respond, I just grilled him and left.

I had the urge to go to club Remi` and see Eternity again. I might have to kill her since she was making me feel shit I normally didn't. I prided myself on being emotionless, not being moved by anyone. But here I was thinking about this girl I had seen for only a few minutes. I was picturing her naked in my bed, her hair spread out on the pillows. Just picturing her pretty face had my dick hard. I didn't want to punish Eternity, I wanted to experience her. Yea, I was going to have to get rid of her much sooner than later.

I parked in Remee's owners spot like I always did once I got to the club, he always talked shit, but I didn't give a fuck. I went back and forth with myself, trying to figure out if I was going in or not. Grabbing my gun, I headed inside. As soon as I made it through the door, the first person I laid eyes on was Deanna. She was looking all sad and shit, but I didn't care. It wasn't stopping nothing I had going on. In a few days, she would be calling me to come bust down her throat. "Yo, set me up in VIP. I want Eternity to serve me." She rolled her eyes, then sighed. "Bitch why are you still standing there? I told you what to do now go fucking do it." She scurried away to do what I wanted.

I didn't need anyone to show me the way to the section we kept for family so I climbed the stairs alone. Once I was settled, I sat back and waited. "Oh, hell no," Eternity commented as soon as she saw it was me. Her reaction was funny to me.

I looked at her and smirked. "Damn girl, that's how you talk to customers?" I saw her have an internal battle between cursing me out and trying to hold on to her job.

"Good evening sir, what can I get you?"

"So, you don't know who I am?" I asked. I was really curious because most people who knew me feared me and she was acting very unafraid. My reputation usually spoke for itself.

"Your Ransom. Yes, I know who you are. It doesn't give you the right to talk to me fucking crazy though. So, if you think that means something to me, it doesn't. Now can I take your drink order? I have other customers to tend to as well."

"Bring me two bottles of Hennessey and four bottles of water. Tell Natalie I said come up here." I saw the fear of being in trouble cross her face briefly, but she wrote down my drink request and went to do her job. She was stronger than she looked, and I admired that. I would never want a woman I could easily break.

"Hello Ransom, what can I do for you tonight?" Natalie had been running my cousins' clubs since day one, and she did a damn good job. She also knew how to keep her pussy closed, which was rare on this scene. She was Rumor's cousin, the only one who she really fucked wit, so it was almost like having family around.

"What's up with Eternity?" I wanted to know more about her.

Natalie threw her hands up in the air and frowned. "Come on

Ransom, not Eternity. She is my best worker. Please don't make her quit." I laughed at her response. "I know you and you never mean these females any good. She isn't like the other girls who work here. She is smart, a nice person and the customers like her."

"You mean the nigga's like her?" I asked feeling anger flow through my body. I was used to being angry, but behind a bitch, nah that was some new shit.

"Yes nigga's like her, she is pretty. She makes your cousin a lot of money and makes my job easier. She is a single mother, comes in and does her job and minds her own business. I will fight you Cahir. I know I can't win but I will try if you fuck this girl up. Walk away from this one. She has been through a lot." Natalie shook her head at me and walked away. All she did was make me want Eternity more. I just wondered how I would get her to fuck wit me.

13

ETERNITY

I LOOKED out my peephole for what felt like the hundredth time, a look of confusion on my face. I know this crazy nigga wasn't stalking me or no shit like that. Opening the door slowly, he patiently waited until he could see my face. "Took you long enough. I thought I was going to have to break in this motherfucker." I tilted my head to the side in confusion.

"Ransom, why the fuck you at my door at three in the morning. Naw, let me rephrase, why the fuck you at my door at all! How you even know where I live?" He stood there, and I could see a bunch of shit flash across his face. One of them was confusion, was he on some medication or something. Maybe he didn't even remember why he followed me home from the club and knocked on my door.

"Shit ma, you want an honest answer, I don't fucking know. I just felt the need to be in your presence." He walked past me and inside my house like I had invited him inside. I watched in horror, and part excitement as he took off his boots and hoodie and then sat on my couch. "Yo Eternity, close the door." Slowly I did just that. I looked down at the faded pajama short set I had on. It used to have pink and purple flowers, but now it looked a little more like grey and white. I just wore it because it was comfortable. My hand went to my head, and I smoothed the loose hairs back into the sloppy ponytail I had thrown in before my shower. Well, at least I was clean.

"Ransom, is there something I can do for you? Maybe someone I can call?" I stood in front of him still not sure what the fuck was going on.

"First off baby girl I ain't drunk or gone off that shit so no you ain't got to call nobody for me. I'm a grown ass man. If you have a bottle of water that would be cool, I will take that." I hurried to the kitchen and grabbed him the water. I was wondering if I had time to stop and text Bella in case this loony motherfucker left me in here stinking. "Damn shorty sit down, turn on a movie or something. You ain't never chilled with a nigga before?"

"Umm, you don't really look like the Netflix and chill type." He smirked but didn't respond. I sat down on the other end of the couch only for him to drag me closer to him. I was damn near in this nigga's lap as I scrolled through my app on the TV trying to find something to watch. Clicking on *All American,* I tried to relax and see what was going to happen next. "Tee, loosen up some ma. I ain't come here to do shit to you. If I was going to kill you, ya scary ass would have been dead already."

"Are you always so fucking rude?" He glared at me and then looked back at the TV.

"I ain't rude lil mama, I just don't say shit to make people feel good. I talk the truth, and never worry how people feel."

"Why do they call you Ransom?"

"Because I've kidnapped some families in exchange for money," he said like it was nothing. He casually drank his water unbothered, and I wondered why that shit made me like him more. Was I attracted to psychos?

"Well, umm ok. What is your real name?" The conversation was interesting even if it was one-sided as fuck.

"Yo, you nosey as fuck. Stop asking me a bunch of shit, I'm trying to relax. Some shit I don't do often. Sit back and enjoy the show." I carefully laid my head on his chest, and he rested his hand on my stomach, causing butterflies to appear. I spent most of the first two episodes looking at Ransom. He really was sexy as fuck, in a dark kind of way. His skin was the color of cocoa, and he kept his hair cut low with deep waves. He was tatted everywhere, on his left hand he had tattooed *kill,* and his right hand was *or be killed.* His eyes were different, like nothing I had ever seen. I couldn't tell if they were light brown or green. Either way, I was enjoying the view. Even the tiny scar above his eyebrow was cute.

Suddenly he looked down and caught me staring. I just knew his mean ass was going to curse me out; instead, he used his free hand to slowly caress my cheek. Suddenly his eyes changed and were the color of gold. He dipped his head closer to mine and lightly kissed me. His lips lingered like he was unsure before he deepened the kiss. When he finished, his eyes were back to being a strange color, and he turned his attention back to the TV like nothing ever happened. Everything he did was so controlled. I wished for a moment I was more like him. Because at this point, I was making a puddle in my panties and my head was foggy just from the feel of his lips.

I must have fallen asleep because I woke up still in his arms, my neck crooked. He did look the most relaxed I had ever seen him and for some reason that made me happy. Even if he was a savage ass nigga, I felt like there was more to him.

"I know ya little ass ain't sleep no more, what you on for the day Tee?" I slowly sat up and rubbed the back of my neck. It had been years since I laid up with a man and my body wasn't used to being in one spot for so long.

"I have to go and pick up my son soon after I go to the gym." I made sure I worked out at least three days a week. I wasn't a stripper, but it was still good to have a stripper body. Bottle girls made most of their money from tips. He nodded at my plans but didn't offer up his. I wasn't surprised he didn't seem like the type to be telling anyone his moves.

After using the bathroom and washing my face and brushing my teeth, I went into the kitchen to make breakfast. "Ransom, you want some food," I asked. He walked up on me and gave me a what the fuck look, like I had asked something stupid.

"Hell nah, I don't eat from broads. Shit, I barely eat at these restaurants. I don't trust no one like that. Hoes be putting shit in nigga's food all the time. Slow poisoning them with eye drops and antifreeze." I wanted to be offended, but he was serious as fuck. So instead I decided to just feel bad for him, that he had that much mistrust in, well, everybody.

"Umm, ok. More for me," I said, and he chuckled low. I could tell he wasn't really the laughing type.

"Aight ma, seeing as how you about to get your little man I'm gonna head out. Come lock the door." And just like that I was all alone and wondering did I dream last night.

☙❧

"ETERNITY, someone in the boss's VIP is requesting you," my co-worker Melanie said grinning.

"Ok, I will go up there now, let me just close out section seven."

"Umm, Natalie said to take seven, and all your other sections. She wants you to go now." Shrugging I turned to see what Remee's VIP wanted. The boss wasn't always here so it could have been his brother or one of his crew. I wasn't mad about giving up any other sections, the top floor VIP's tipped way more, and it was pretty slow tonight. As soon as I walked up, I noticed Ransom sitting there, he had his hood up, but his tattoos gave him away. The VIP was dim, the lights turned down, and he had two half-naked girls dancing on him. I hadn't seen him since the night at my house a few days ago, and I found that he had invaded my mind. I was hoping he would have stopped by again because I was missing him. And it wasn't like I had a number to call and see what he was up too. I even wondered was he ok, since in this crazy ass world anything can happen. But looking at him now, he seemed to be more than ok and not interested in fucking wit me.

I wasn't sure why the fuck he wanted me to serve him, and he was up here with two random hoes. It kind of stung seeing him with the other girls after the other night, but shit it wasn't like we had anything going on. And he made it pretty clear he wasn't interested.

"Hello, what can I get for you tonight," I said, making sure I sounded super professional. I enjoyed my job, and I wasn't letting any nigga affect my coins. Slowly he lifted his head I could see by his bloodshot eyes he was already drinking. I noticed the empty bottles at the far end of the table and wondered how long he had been here. Something about the look on his face made me wonder was he ok.

"Clear out," he barked at the two females. When they didn't move fast enough, he shoved them out of the way, causing one to stumble over the other. I tried not to laugh, but those bitches looked like naked clowns the way they were falling all over each other. The thing that wasn't so funny was the look of fear on their faces while they struggled to get the fuck out of the section.

"Ransom, can I get you something?" I asked, moving closer to him.

"Yea, just come chill wit a nigga." He said as he sat up from the plush couch.

"I'm working right now, so I really can't chill while on the clock. Let me see if I can take my break and I can give you fifteen minutes." I was willing to give him my little bit of free time because I could sense something was going on with him. Normally I would have told him how he disgusted me with those hoes, but for once I bit my tongue.

"You don't need to use your break ma, but that's fucking real that you would give up your time for me. Natalie knows your spending the rest of your shift up here. I just need..." He stopped like he was afraid to say that he needed a damn thing from anyone. "Yo just sit down, you want a drink?"

I knew Natalie was sick of this nigga pulling me off the job for his own personal needs. But it wasn't like it was my fault. "Ok, what you drinking," I said as I gingerly sat next to him. I went to sneak a look at the bottles, but he was already pouring some of the Patron in the cup. I had a feeling he had been drinking straight from the empty bottles. He handed it to me, and I took it and stared.

"Ransom, where the hell is my chaser?"

"Come on Tee, you weak as fuck for that ma. Take it to the head." He smirked at me as I drank the Patron straight. That shit had my eyes burning, I wasn't a huge drinker normally. But tonight I sat upstairs drinking all types of shit with him. It wasn't even midnight, and I was drunk as fuck. Even though he had way more than me, his demeanor never changed. "Yo get you a water, I ain't trying to take ya ass home, and you throw up in my whip. I will put you out and make you walk. I'm just going to follow behind to make sure you good." I hurried and drank the Fiji water that he had in the section wondering why the fuck he thought I was going home with him.

"Aight, it's time to roll," he said as soon as I finished the bottle. I looked around being dramatic as fuck.

"Who is going where with who? I ain't bout to leave wit you." He ignored my little antics and stood up. He left a few stacks on the table and pulled me up with him.

"Like I said it's time to go." He led me down the stairs, holding my waist the whole time, so I didn't stumble like a fucking drunk. Before we made it to the door, I stopped in my tracks. "Shorty what now?"

"I got to pee," I whined glancing at the bathroom. I felt all eyes on the two of us and wondered if leaving with him was a good idea. I had a feeling this was against a lot of rules in the employee handbook.

He laughed slightly showing his grill. "Cool, do ya thing."

Letting me go I went in the bathroom before I had an accident. Those drinks were catching up to me and fast. I handled my business and washed my hands. Splashing some cold water on my face, I felt a little better. I turned to leave and almost ran into one of my co-workers. Some hood rat named Deanna.

"Wow Eternity, you going home to fuck Ransom? Let me give you some advice. First of all, that dick belongs to me. When you're sucking him off, those are my pussy juices your tasting. Oh, and if you haven't heard, he likes it rough, really rough," she said smirking and pointing to the fingerprints around her neck. I also noticed the trail of bite marks on the top of her breasts that were visible in her low-cut shirt.

"Umm thanks," I murmured as I damn near fled the bathroom. Deanna snickered as she followed behind me. Before I could even tell Ransom I changed my mind, he had picked up on that shit.

"The fuck wrong wit you," he snapped. I wondered if this nigga ever just spoke to people in a normal tone of voice.

Shaking my head, I subconsciously looked Deanna's way. "Nothing, I just need to get home." Seconds later, he had Deanna shoved against the wall with a gun to her head.

"Jealous hoes catch hot ones. The fuck you say to her?" He was clicking, and I wondered was he about to blow her brains out in front of me. I grew up in the hood and had seen some gruesome shit, but this nigga just wasn't all there. I watched him closely and I saw a glimpse of something that looked like regret when his eyes met mine.

"Bae I was just telling her how you liked to be fucked. I didn't want you to be disappointed." The gun went from her head to being shoved in her mouth. I grimaced seeing the look of pain cross her face.

"Come on Ransom, you can't be doing that shit in here," one of the security guards named Luke said as he walked over to us.

The look on Ransom's face was comical, and if Luke was smart, he would have kept it moving and not be a captain save a hoe. "Shit homie, I can do whatever the fuck I want in this bitch. What you think you going to do about it? I mean I'm ready to see you try, come on nigga don't just stand there. Come and make me leave this bitch alone." Luke backed up when he noticed the light hit the chrome piece in his hand. "Yea, I thought so pussy ass mother fucker. Now in the future mind, your business before your wife is picking out a black dress. Her name is Tricia right? Her pussy was loose but the head was aight." I could feel his anger escalating, and I knew I had to get him out of there before there ended up being a pile of dead bodies. The fact his mouth had no filter definitely didn't help the situation.

Timidly I walked over and touched his hand. "Come on Ransom, let's go," I urged. I was scared as fuck he would be turning his gun on me next, but I had to at least try and calm him down. Surprisingly when he turned to look down at me, his gaze softened, and he stepped back.

"Next time, there won't be a next time Deanna," he said, giving her a warning. She looked at me with gratefulness, but I just mugged her. This shit could have been avoided if she wasn't being a bitch. We got outside and I remembered I had driven to work so I couldn't just leave my car. I knew I was lit because how else had I gotten to work.

"Ransom, I can't just leave my car," I said staring at my '07 Camry. It wasn't much, but it got me everywhere I needed to go.

"You can get it tomorrow. I will make sure they don't tow it." I followed him to his car, the tints on the Audi were so dark they blended in with the black paint job. All the darkness of the vehicle suited him. I opened my own door once he hit the alarm, I could tell he wasn't the type to be opening doors and shit. He drove with his gun in his lap, and I realized he stayed ready. He was the kind of nigga I should be afraid of, but for some reason I was intrigued. I looked up shocked when I realized he had pulled up in front of my condo, I assumed he was taking me to his place. It really didn't matter to me, so I didn't bother mentioning it.

I got out and unlocked the door, but he stood in the front entryway. "Your son home?" he asked an odd look on his face.

"No, why what's up?"

"Cool, I don't fuck wit kids like that." He said as he walked inside. I felt my heart sink when he said that. I could never have a real future with someone who couldn't or wouldn't be around my son. I would have never guessed he didn't like kids after the way he interreacted with Cassian the day I met him. "Come on ma, a nigga tired as fuck," he fussed from the bottom of the stairs. I locked up and went over to him. Once we got upstairs, I showed him my room before I went to shower. I was nervous after hearing what Deanna had to say, and I hoped I didn't regret bringing Ransom home. I finished brushing my teeth and threw on a pair of colorful boy shorts and sports bra from Ethika. I didn't know what to do with my hair, so I brushed it up into a sleek ponytail.

I stood at the bedroom door, watching him. I never realized how tall he was until now. He had to be at least six foot three because he made my queen-sized bed look small as fuck. He was laid back in only a pair of Armani boxers, he made sure his gun was on the bedside table next to him. His eyes were so low I thought he was asleep until he motioned for me to come here with his hand. Slowly I walked to the edge of the bed, my nerves were getting the best of me. I had only been with one man since my son's father, and he was nothing like Ransom.

"Eternity, I don't want you to be scared of me," he said as his hand ran over my bare stomach. He lightly ran his fingers over my belly rings, I had the top and bottom of my belly button pierced.

"I thought that was what you do, instill fear into people." I had no idea where that shit came from, but I wished I would have shut the fuck up.

He didn't answer just pulled me on the bed, so I was straddling him. I could feel his dick grow under me, and I almost fainted. No wonder he got me drunk before he took me home. He was huge and I knew I couldn't hang. Before I could panic too much, he snatched my hair out of the ponytail and grabbed a handful. Once he had a good grip, he eased my head closer until I could feel his breath on my face. He kissed me and just off of that I was horny. Why did everything about him turn me on.

I slipped my tongue in his mouth, and he tasted like liquor and mints. I have no idea how long we kissed or when he popped my breasts out of the sports bra, I had on, but suddenly he was sucking my nipples. That shit had me wet as fuck. I was embarrassed because I knew he could feel me dripping all over him. "Take this shit off," he demanded as he helped me tug my clothes off. He rolled me onto my back and just looked me up and down. I wanted to cover all my girly parts from his intense gaze. He took his hand and ran it up my leg and stopped right before he got to my pussy. I was thanking God that I waxed even though I didn't have a man. His fingers brushed my clit, and I moaned.

By the time he was done playing with my pussy, I had come at least twice. "Ransom, please," I begged just wanting to feel him inside of me.

He took off his boxers, and I automatically scooted up on the bed running from his dick. It wasn't just long it was thick, the veins throbbing on either side. "Don't run shorty, this what you crying for and shit." What I thought would equal pain ended up being the best feeling I had ever experienced. He entered me slowly and kissed me at the same time. I ran my hands over his chest, fascinated with every inch of him. He lightly bit my neck, then sucked on it after every bite. I knew I was going to have marks all over my body the next day.

I moaned into his mouth and started bucking my hips so I could take more of him. When he went hard and gave me all the dick, I screamed his name. Suddenly he stopped moving and looked into my eyes. "Stop calling me that shit, it ain't for you. My name is Cahir."

I was stunned, I wasn't expecting that from him. He grabbed my ass and pulled me closer to him, causing my legs to open even more. He sucked on my breast, and I felt something I never felt before. It was like I was having an out of body experience. "Cahir, don't stop," I cried out. He went harder, giving me what I wanted, and I felt my body shudder. No wonder Deanna was lying on him, this was the best dick I ever had.

"Tee, come wit me ma," he commanded causing my body to instantly react. I felt him nut inside of me, and I didn't have time to even think about the possible consequences. I came with him, and for the first time ever, I saw something besides anger in his eyes.

❧ 14 ❧

RUMOR

"Mommy, call daddy now! Please," my daughter demanded shoving her iPad in my face. At three years old A'Laya Remi` Frances was the cutest, smartest and most spoiled little girl I had ever known. And the largest cause of her being spoiled was on the other end of the Factime call she was asking me to make. Remee didn't lie when he said he would love A'Laya like she was his own. His whole family loved her, she was considered the first grandchild, and first niece and if she crooked her chubby little finger the McKenzie clan came running. Somedays I wanted to scream at all of them, but I was mostly just grateful she had a family to love on her.

I hit the button and waited while the phone rung. "Hey daddy's angel," Remee answered fast as hell. I listened to the two of them talk about her birthday party next weekend and damn near choked on my water when I heard him mention a pony. Before I could address the issue I saw a girl come into the camera.

"Hey Remee, can we chill," she cooed damn near in his ear and I felt my stomach twist into knots. Lately we had fell into a routine. He didn't live with me but he was at my condo every night unless he was handling business. I hadn't even seen a bunch of bitch's calling his phones. I thought maybe he was settling down. But I guess I was wrong. I couldn't be angry, Rem told me he couldn't be my man. He was clear on the fact he was going to keep being a hoe. He never made me any false promises.

"Girl, get the fuck away from me. I'm on the phone with my kid and I aint interested, now move around." He sounded mad and I couldn't tell if it was just because he was talking to Laya or because he really wasn't interested. I sighed and went in the other room so I could mind my business.

"Mommy," A'Laya called running into the room her iPad facing me. "Daddy said come here." She giggled like the two of them were in on some fucking private joke.

"What Rem," I said with an attitude.

"What the fuck you made for? You miss this dick?" He said causing me to blush and cover Laya's ears.

"Remee, ya mouth nigga damn. And no I don't miss it. Matter of fact I'm about to put her down for a nap and get on one of those dating sites so I can find some new D-I-C-K." All the laughter stopped on his end and his face was scowling. Yea that nigga was mad as fuck. I never talked about other men or dating so he had gotten comfortable. And even though I was just fucking wit him now I was enjoying pushing his buttons.

"Rumor, don't play wit me ma. I swear you don't want me hunting down these internet niggas and pushing they shit back."

"Bye A'Remee!!! Layla, tell daddy bye bye," I urged causing her to blow him kisses and wave. I hung up on him because he was still talking shit. I was laughing so hard at his reaction I was damn near in tears. I had learned to deal with our non committed situation in my own way, a way that didn't leave me broken at the end of the day. "Come on Layla, nap time." I swear I was the only one that used my baby's actual name. His whole family called her little Remi` because of her middle name. She smiled at me and went to get her pink blankey.

After laying her down on her princess bed I took a quick shower so I could relax. I wasn't usually home on a weekday, but

I took a week off to prepare for her Birthday party. Even though Remee gave me enough money and then some I kept a part time job at a call center. I hated dealing with the angry customers, most complaining about their cell phone bill. But I needed to make my own money. I just started my last year of college for my Bachelors in social work. Even though I needed a Masters for my career to take off I wasn't sure I could keep juggling school, child and work. So I may make this year my last.

I lotioned my skin and put on a Nike sports bra and matching shorts. I grabbed my phone and laid on my bed to scroll. I must have fallen asleep because I woke up to Remee on the bed over me. He placed his knee in between my legs forcing them open as he placed kisses down my back. I tried to roll over onto my back but he held me down. "What was that hot shit you was talking Rumor?"He snatched my phone and started checking my DM's. I smirked when he saw all the niggas trying to shoot their shot. "Man, what the fuck is going on. Who all these clown ass dudes. Rumor you better not be responding to these nigga's either."

He threw my phone down and turned me over so I was facing him. I could barely focus with his big dick grinding up against my clit. "Nah Ru, don't be trying to get at my man now. The dick is off limits, ya ass on fucking punishment." He sucked on my neck and brushed his fingers over my pussy lips.

"How the fuck I'm being punished and I aint did shit," I whined. "Matter of fact, if I wanted to talk to another nigga so fucking what! You aint my man." I was low key about to get mad since I couldn't get none.

Instead of clapping back at me he stopped to look me in my eyes. "Don't say that shit Rumor. I'm ya nigga, you don't need nobody else. I put you first, show you love. Don't do this shit right now, I can't take it. I need you, hold on a little while longer. I promise I'm about to change this shit for the better." He finished his sentence with a kiss that took my breath away. Before I could think about what he was saying he was dicking me down. It was just as good as always, he had me arching my fucking back like a cat and screaming like a victim of some sorts. "I love you Rumor, I swear I love you," Remee said. He grabbed my hips and I couldn't hold back anymore. I came and collapsed below him to finish the sleep he had interrupted.

15

REMEE

"Damn nigga, lil sis got yo ass in love." Sire joked as he looked at the ring box I had opened and set on the desk.

"Yea, Amira did good picking that shit out. I know Rumor is going to love it. But ar you sure about this? Marriage is forever, or at least until you kill your spouse to break free." I shook my head and just stared at Cahir for a second. This nigga was ruthless and I was sorry whatever women some day learned to love him. "I get it though, good pussy fucks ya head up. Man shorty from your club be having me slipping. I ran up in old girl raw the other day." He looked sad as fuck that he did that shit.

"Son when the fuck you did that shit? You talking about Eternity? Man don't get that girl pregnant, she cannot survive you for eighteen years and Natalie will kill both of us if you ruin her employee."

"The first time was the night my mother died." He stopped and ran his hand over his face and I wondered what Eternity was doing to my cousin, because it seemed like she was breaking down some of his walls. I was shocked he even told us about that shit. "Man we not fucking talking abuot me, we talking about your ass turning in your players card!" Him and Sire fell out laughing.

"Shit it's time man. Rumor deserve this shit and more, shorty done put up with way to much from a nigga like me." They nodded in agreement and I looked at the white gold engagement ring lined with diamonds. I was ready to marry Rumor, give her a few more babies. I realized I couldn't do this shit with out her and I didn't want to. So tomorrow at our daughter's birthday I was going to pop the question. I just prayed she says yes and doesn't make me get fucking ignorant.

"Remee, I'm sorry to bother you but there is someone downstairs requesting to speak to you. She is refusing to leave and basically causing a scene," Natalie announced standing In my office doorway. I knew it had to be serious if she didn't just handle it herself. Shoving the ring back in my pocket I grabbed my gun of the desk and made my way downstairs.

"Can I help you," I said to the woman who had her back turned. As soon as she faced me my heart sank.

"Hey baby daddy. I've missed you," Jayda cooed as she rubbed her protruding belly. This bitch looked like she was ready to pop any second now and I literally felt myself sweating bullets. I could still see the scene in my head like a horror film. Me pulling out of her pussy to find a busted condom. But I checked in with her, she said she wasn't pregnant. I asked a few fucking times and this bitch bold face lied. "I can see by the look on your face you have put two and two together. Yes it's yours, yes nigga I lied, and yes it is way to late for a fucking abortion." She laughed and it took all of my strength not to kill her.

"Bitch you have to be fucking kidding. Just tell me this shit is a joke right now. What you want money? I got you, name your price, just tell me that aint my fucking kid." I couldn't do this shit to Rumor. Not right now, I was finally about to do right.

"Oh Remee, I don't want your money. I want you, and I mean all of you. I been hearing around the way that you and Rumor are exclusive now. You cut all. Your bitches off for her. But guess what, you are going to leave her. If you don't I will make her life hell. I mean drive byes, pop ups, slashing tires and faces. I will go to no lengths to make sure you belong to me." She gave me an evil grin and I started to think about killing a pregnant woman. Even if she was carrying my baby.

"Well we only have a few weeks left. It's a boy, the son she never could give you. I will send the details for my baby shower you and your family can throw me, the push gift I want and the last few doctors appointment. Whatever Rumor got, I want ten times better! Love you baby daddy. See you really soon." She blew me a kiss and strolled out without a care in the world, when she just ruined mine.

❦

I WATCHED my daughter ride the pony with the fake unicorn horn on its head around Powder Mills Park, her in the front and Tayri in the back. Her party was lit and everyone I knew with kids, plus her whle pre-school class was there. The slip and slides and bounce houses were popular. "Babe, you overdid it. Why is there a snow cone machine? I know she aint ask for half this shit," Rumor said as she came to stand in front of me. Automatically my arms went around her and she melted into my chest. Since I told her to give me a chance the other day, shit had been so good. And now it was all about to fucked up. Gently I kissed her forehead and she looked up and me and smiled. "Rem, I'm really happy right now. I see you coming through and I appreciate you. I love you A'Remee."

Every word was like a knife to my chest. I literally was having trouble breathing. "I love you to ma. Don't ever forget that shit." I held her tighter, wanting to keep her with me forever. I knew I had to tell her about messy ass Jayda, before Jayda did. She deserved that from me. The party went by to fast. I was dreading the end of the day. When we got to my mom's house to drop off A'Laya I knew I had to break it off with Rumor now.

"Yo Ru, I need to talk to you out here," I said as everyone else went in the kitchen. Everyone was giving me an excited ass look as they left us alone in the living room. I realized that once again I would be hurting my family as well as Rumor.

"You ok Remee, you don't loo so good. If your sick we can go home now, we don't have to chill." She put her hand on mine and gave me a look of concern. Slowly I moved her hand off of mine and stepped back.

"Ma look, I got some shit to tell you. I can't fuck wit you anymore Ru. It aint shit you did, this all on me. I swear this wasn't how this shit was supposed to go. But I can't hurt you again." It had been years since I seen this much pain on her face. "I'm so sorry Rumor," I said low. I could tell she heard me though by the way the anger lept in her eyes.

"So it's true. She DM'd me on IG. Told me about ya'll son," she said and started crying.

"Mommy, don't cry. Daddy, why is mommy crying?" A'Laya asked from the doorway.

I watched as Rumor's eyes landed on Laya and they seemed stuck. I watched a bunch of emotions cross her face, one being regret. "I get it now, it's because of her, your leaving me because I had a baby with another man. Your leaving for a girl who can give you a baby of your own." I had never felt this much anger towards Rumor. I slammed her against the wall so hard her head bounced.

"Don't you ever in your fucking life put my daughter in this shit. Why would you say that dumb shit Rumor. Why the fuck you looking at my daughter with regret. I love her more than any fucking body, I will fuck you up about her," I seethed. Letting her go I punched a hole in the wall that caused her and Laya to scream.

"What the fuck is going on out here," my mother said as she rushed in the room. Amira, Sire and Cahir behind her. "Amira, take A'Laya out of here."

"No, give me my daughter she is going home with me," Rumor yelled as she reached out for her.

"Move. My fucking kid aint going nowhere wit ya retarded

ass." I snatched Laya from my sister and went upstairs to my room. I could still hear the screams from Rumor as she bawled. Her heart broken. "Daddy's so sorry baby," I whispered into my daughter's curls as she cried herself to sleep in my arms, my tears mixing with hers.

❧ 16 ❧

CAHIR

I WATCHED as she followed the other two girls into VIP, all of them carrying bottles, the fire spitting from the sparklers they used. Typically I would have been checking to see who had the fattest ass out of the group. Instead, I only saw her. She looked sexy as fuck in the little black shorts and tight black shirt that had the Remi`s logo on the front. Her hair was in some long braids down her back. The little gold charms matching her gold hoops and gold belly rings. I was mad as fuck when I saw all these little niggas watching her, but I couldn't show it. I didn't even know where this shit came from. I wasn't the type of nigga who cared. And I wasn't about to change just because shorty had good pussy. Even if it was the best I ever had. Ever since the first time I just couldn't get enough and I stayed creeping in shorty's bed anytime her son wasn't home. Sometimes we just chilled and didn't even fuck.

They set the bottles and buckets down on the tables before turning to leave. I noticed Eternity hesitate a little as she looked up and gave me a shy smile. Instead of responding, I grabbed the bottle of Hennessy I requested and took it to the head. Her smile faded, but she still made sure everyone had what they needed. "Yo Eternity," Sire called out before she could leave.

"Hey Sire, you need anything else?" She shouted over the loud music.

"Nah, I'm straight. Hold this," he said as he handed a few blue faces her way. Before the money even touched her hand, I could see Roneika's messy ass elbowing Shay.

"Thank y-" Eternity started before Shay jumped up, hands fisted ready to swing.

"Sire, you fucking around with this bitch? I'm so fucking sick of you. For real, the hoe you been creeping with works in your brother's club. Then you want to low key tip her ass! Hell, overtip her, How fucking convenient!" Shay was doing the most, hands waving, breasts damn near falling out of her come fuck me dress. My cousin really picked a fucking winner. He would have been better off bringing Bella. Shorty was broke as fuck, but she knew how to act right.

"Mane shut the hell up with that shit. This why I don't bring yo ass out, you ignorant as fuck. Your little pet too," he said nodding to Roneika. All the niggas laughed, but she so fucking stupid she laughed with them. I knew Roneika ass was dumb from the few times I fucked her.

"No, I ain't sitting down, this brave bitch still standing here looking stuck. You fucking my man? Do his dick taste good? That's the only thing you can offer him that I can't, you not even that fucking cute." I saw Eternity step back and get a crazy look on her face. As much as I wouldn't mind seeing Tee whoop Shay's ass, I knew she was on her job and shit.

"Yo Shay, shut the fuck up." I seethed letting her know her shit was done. She sat down and folded her arms like a spoiled child. But she got the fucking point. Now Roneika was busy grilling me like she could check my ass. I was looking forward to beating her silly if she even tried.

"Well damn shorty, if you bussin it open for niggas like that let me hit summin." This nigga named Jax said as he let his eyes roam all over Eternity's body. Half the team was calling out to her, asking for her number. Sire looked at me to see if I was going to respond, but he knew better. I mugged the fuck out of him. She wasn't my girl, so this shit wasn't any of my fucking business. I was annoyed that he knew I was fucking her because now he thought I was about to turn into captain save a hoe.

"Umm, no thank you. I'm good," she responded, her eyes snapping but her tone even.

"Fuck you bitch, you think you're too good for me? What a nigga ain't got enough money for you, yo pussy only reserved for boss niggas. Fucking ugly duck ass hoe. I just wanted to nut all over your face anyway. Shit, I thought you would be grateful for the fucking attention." She looked up at me, and I saw the hurt all over her face. I felt that shit to my fucking soul, the soul I didn't even know still existed. It was getting harder to just sit there and watch her be mistreated.

"Nah, I bet you fucking tonight bitch," Mikey said as he got up and grabbed her pussy.

"Nigga get off of me," she cried out damn near falling on the floor trying to get away from him. She didn't have to bother because the moment I saw his hands on her, I couldn't sit there anymore.

"Nigga don't ever put your fucking hands on her again," I roared as I let my fists connect with his face. I felt his jaw crunch, and I knew his shit was broken. After the first hit, I couldn't stop myself. Blood was coming from all over, and his face was unrecognizable. But all I could see was him touching her body. She belonged to me.

"Aight son, that nigga damn near dead. Ease up some," Sire said looking at Mikey's mangled body. Before I could start fucking him up next, Remee came upstairs.

"What the fuck ya'll niggas up in my shit doing?" I know he wanted to ask me what I was doing but wouldn't in front of all these people. "Dame, clean this shit up and get this nigga out of here."

"Dame, take care of that permanently," I said, letting him know I wanted Mikey dead.

"Yo Rem, let me holla at you for a second cuz." Eternity dropped her head and backed away towards the stairs. "The fuck you going shorty," I barked as I grabbed her. I could tell she was upset just by the way her body went stiff when I touched her. "Come on Tee, you mad for what ma? I just beat the fuck out of that nigga behind you and you in your feelings? Sit ya ass down." I damn near shoved her into the spot I was sitting in and went to holla at my cousin. I gave Sire a look, so he knew to make sure she was good.

I followed him in the back to his office and paced the room like a caged animal. "What's that shit all about? You been fucking wit shorty or something?" See this was the shit I didn't want. "Son for real you just had Mikey killed behind a girl no one knows you fucking wit?" He was chuckling like this shit was funny.

"Don't fucking worry about it. But I don't want her ass working the VIP no more. Put her behind the bar or fire her. These niggas disrespectful as hell. And make her wear pants, not those little ass shorts." This nigga smirked, and I wanted to break his jaw next.

"Don't put ya fucking hands on me kid, because if you do, I'm fighting ya ass back." He left out, and I sat there for a few minutes, just trying to get my head together. I couldn't believe I was doing all this shit for some girl I was smashing.

As soon as I made it back to VIP, I noticed Mikey's bloody corpse was picked up like nothing even happened. Roneika walked over to me and slithered her body close to mine. "Baby, I can see you are angry. Why don't you come and take it out on me," she cooed in her sexiest voice? Normally I would have jumped at the chance to fuck her in every hole, enjoying her screams, her begging me to stop. But lately, all I wanted was to hear Eternity begging me not to stop, to watch her face bawl up in pleasure because I was inside of her. I hated that she was changing me, but I couldn't deny it.

I pushed her ass, "get the fuck off me yo. If I want to fuck, I will let you know. Don't be approaching me and don't be doing all that because of shorty." Her smile was immediately wiped from her face.

"Fuck that bitch, all she going to get from you is the same as the rest of us. A stiff dick and a face filled with nut." She was so sure of herself, and normally I would agree. But if Roneika only fuckin knew what Eternity was getting, she would probably kill herself.

"Really Cahir, you got me demoted? Like what the fuck did I ever do to deserve meeting a nigga like you," Eternity said as she got in my face. Her face was stained with tears, and her fists were bawled up like she wanted to hit me. The thought of her hitting me caused me to chuckle low. "Oh, I'm a joke now, right?"

"Bitch you been a fucking joke. He doesn't care about you, and Ransom and I were holding a conversation. So, if you don't mind move around." Roneika damn near shoved Eternity as she waved her long ass fingernails.

"Bitch, fuck you. I will move around when I'm done. And if you don't want me to break your fucking fingers, keep your hands out of my face." My little baby was mad as fuck, her caramel colored skin was a deep red, and she was ready to light Roneika's ass up. I wasn't about to let Eternity fight Roneika though. That hoe didn't fight fair, I could already see the lights bounce off the blade she had in her hand.

Grabbing her by the throat, I lifted her in the air. "I don't know why every fucking body wants to try me tonight but this ain't what it is. Had you even moved that blade in her direction, you would be dead. Now instead of choking on my dick, you just choking." I waited until she almost passed out before I dropped her to the ground. "Eternity, let's go," I said, picking up a new Henny bottle on the way out. I grabbed her arm, but she gave me the coldest look I had ever seen before she snatched away and ran down the stairs. *Fuck.* As much as I shouldn't care, I didn't want her mad at me.

Coming up behind her once I got outside, I wrapped my arms around her, and for the first time all night, I felt good. I couldn't lie, I loved when she was close to me. "Get off of me. I don't need you saving me, so you didn't have to do all of that. And I sure as fuck ain't going nowhere with you. Maybe you should go back inside for Roneika, I'm sure she would still be willing." Hell, I was sure she would be too.

"Tee, don't be mad at me, come on ma," I pleaded as I kissed her on her neck. I had to be drunk as fuck, this wasn't me.

"Don't be mad at you? Nigga, are you mixing cocaine with that Henny? You don't give a fuck about me, so let's not pretend. Do you know I make more per hour as a bottle girl than a bartender and that my tips are better? I depend on that money to pay my bills and now thanks to you I have to get a second job. You had no right to tell Remee that shit. This is my fucking lively hood." She shoved me, but she was so small compared to me I didn't move.

"I did what the fuck I had to, what you want me in here wilding out on these niggas every night? This shit ain't even me. You want these nigga's blood on your hands?"

"I could have handled it myself. You could have shut it down before it even got that far, but I'm just some girl you fucking. Not important enough for you to be bothered with.

She was sobbing by now, her body shaking, and her eyes swollen. I thought about her son, and the fact I just basically took food out his mouth and that shit didn't sit right with me. I didn't know how to be around people and not be selfish, and this just proved it. Picking her up, I walked to my truck and put her inside. Shorty was fighting me the whole time, not saying shit but her fists were flying. Once I slammed the door, she sunk against it in defeat. I stood outside, running my hands over my waves. How the fuck I even get here, this was some Remee and Rumor type shit.

I drove to her spot and parked, she had cried herself to sleep, and that shit had me angry inside. I did that, made her sad, and for a minute I thought about just dropping her off and getting the fuck out of here. "Ma, wake up, we here." I shook her gently, causing her to jump up. She grabbed her keys out of her purse and got out. I followed behind, and even though she didn't say shit, she just kept looking at me cutting her eyes. As soon as we made it inside, she took off all her clothes. My dick had never been so hard, shorty was perfect, her body was more than a ten. She stalked upstairs, and I could hear the shower running. Going to her bedroom, I took off my Timbs and hoodie then set on the edge of her bed to wait for her.

She came from the bathroom smelling like that sweet shit she always had on. Even though I liked it, I made a mental note to buy her some Gucci perfume next time I hit the mall. She deserved it. "Can you just get it over with so you can get the hell out of my life." My head shot up, what the fuck was she talking about? I hoped she knew I wasn't going nowhere.

"Get what over with shorty?" I asked as she moved to stand in front of me.

"Just hurry and fuck me, so you can leave." She sounded tired, and I didn't even mean tired from the day I mean tired of life, tired of me. That shit had a nigga feeling something I ain't felt since I was a kid, scared. I stood up and pushed her back a little. I took off my t-shirt and put it over her body because if I kept looking at her naked, she would be on the bed spreadeagle. I had to get away from her, I didn't do this feelings shit. The fact I was scared of losing her meant she was a liability I couldn't afford.

"Shorty I ain't never fucked ya ass, trust that ain't for you. Hell, you can barely manage the dick, the fuck I look like going through all this shit for some mediocre pussy." Her face crumpled, and the pain in her eyes had me weak as fuck, but I had to make her hate me. "I swear bitch's like you will have a nigga caught the fuck up out here. Throwing yourself in front of me like I been raping you or something." Turning to get my hoodie and boots, I heard her sobbing behind me. I wanted to apologize, go wipe her tears away. But I had to get shorty out of my system. "Yo Eternity, don't hit my fucking line again," I snapped as I walked out of the room.

17

SIRE

I ROLLED over to my phone going off back to back and I knew it was Shay. Lately I barely tried to hide the fact I was cheating on her. Whatever me and her had was a mistake and now that I had Arabella back in my life, I needed to find a way out of that shit. Instead of answering her call I shot her a text asking what the fuck she wanted. I wasn't worried about my daughter because last I knew she was with my mother. That was some regular shit. Shay enjoyed running the streets and spending my money, the only time she was quiet was when my dick was in her mouth.

"Babe you good," Bella said as she lifted her head off the pillow and smiled at me. I felt bad for waking her up with my phone. Her smile was still everything, especially now, because it reached her eyes thee days. Killing Alex was long overdue. When I found out what he had done to her I couldn't wait a minute longer to get at him. And it was worth it, my shorty was sleeping good as fuck at night. Even though I didn't confirm what I had did I think she knew what was up. Or maybe it was just because I was here most nights and she knew I was going hard as fuck for her.

"Yea babe I'm always good when I'm wit you." I felt my head pound when my phone went off back to back again. I checked the messages and felt like shit. I had forgot today was my baby girl's doctors appointment. She was seeing an allergist for testing because something was making her break out all the fucking time. I let Shay know I was on the way and sat up. I was frustrated with my whole fucking situation, Bella was off today and I was looking forward to laying up. But my little one had to come first. I just wished Bella was her mom instead of Shay retarded ass.

"Bells, I got some business that just came up. So I'm gonna slide throught tonight after dinner?" If Bella noticed we didn't go out much she never commented. She was really pretty easy going. I honestly didn't give a fuck if Shay knew about Bella, but I didn't want to run into Shay's ratchet ass friends while we were out. They would for sure make sure Bella knew I had a woman.

"Ok Sire, no problem. I am going to just relax since Eternity has Jael. If you want me to cook something for you later just let me know." She got on her knees and looked up so I could kiss her. Bella was sweet, she didn't fuss about anything and was just happy to be in my presence. The only thing she had every really asked of me was to someday meet my mom since she said we seemed close.

I headed out and drove the thirty minutes from Greece to Henrietta. I made good time and I was happy to see we would make the appointment on time. I blew the horn hoping my daughter was dressed properly and Shay ass looked like a mother and not a streetwalker. Shay came out with a pair of skin tight jeans on and a cropped sweater. Her long weave was platium blonde today and straight down her back. She was pretty, with curves in all the right places, but her insides were fucking ugly.

"Whats up baby daddy. I see you found your way home for a day." She said talking shit once she got in the front seat.

"Man Shay, shut the fuck up. This the reason I don't come around. You annoying as fuck. Grow up if you want me to come around." Even as I said that I knew it was a lie. She could become the best mother since Claire Huckstable and I wouldn't want to com around. I was in love with Bella. I think I always had been.

"Whats up Tay Tay," I called out to my daughter causing her to giggle.

"Daddy," she replied giving me a big grin. The doctors office wasn't far away so luckily we only had to be in the car together for about ten minutes. I parked in front of the medical building and turned the truck off. I got Tayari out of her seat in the back and carried her inside. Shay's slow ass was still sitting in the whip texting.

The wait wasn't long before the doctor called us back. "Well Mr. McKenzie, Miss Lee, we could not find any new allergies. Tayari is still only allergic to milk. Is there someone who could possibly be giving her milk unknowingly?" My eyes shifted to Shay and just like I thought she looked guilty as fuck.

"Shay please tell me you aint been giving my daughter cows milk?" I was trying to remain calm but she had me pissed off.

"Well I can't always find the almond milk so I just give her the regular. I don't see what the big deal is," she said sounding dumb as fuck.

"Thanks Doctor, we will handle it from here." I got my baby girl ready to leave and Shay followed. As soona as we got outside and strapped my daughter in the truck I turned on her. "I swear to God you a real foul ass bitch. Just fucking lazy! Shay I'm warning you, this ya last chance when it comes to my daughter."

"Nigga, you not even around, I'm stuck in that big ass house with her all alone. I need a fucking break.She is annoying, I didn't sign up for this! I feel like a single mom." This bitch was still running her fucking mouth as I drove towards the house.

"Fwench fwies," my baby called out as she noticed the Burger King on the right hand side. "Daddy, pleas," she begged. Even though it wasn't Bella's Burger King I felt akward as fuck rolling through with Shay in the car.

"Sire stop so we can feed her or she is going to start bawling." Sure enough I could see the tears in her eyes.

I pulled into the parking lot since the drive thru was out into the road. "Man hurry the fuck up, I got shit to do."

"So you not coming in with us? You act like you can't take thrity minutes from your fucking day and spend with your kid!" My daughter was excited as fuck when she saw she was about to get her favorite snack and I felt guilty. I had been spending less time with her lately. Not because of Bella, but because of Shay. Being around her makes me crazy. I just nodded and got out to grab my baby.

Shay looped her arm in mine when walked in and I was annoyed. She always did this shit in public because she wanted every female walking to know she was my girl. "Babe, I promise I will do better with Tayari. I'm really sorry," she said close to my ear so only I can hear. Except I could barely hear shit. It felt like thr world had turned upside down and there was a buzzing sound in my head. Behind the counter was Arabella. I wanted to back up and run the fuck up out this shit. She was just home a few hours ago, in bed naked. She didn't even work at this location. I had to be tripping. "Sire do you hear me," Shay shouted to get my attention, but I couldn't answer her. Arabella looked up and her eyes met mine. She looked from me to Shay, her face was filled with confusion, then hurt and I knew I had fucked up.

18

RUMOR

I STARED at the book in front of me and read the same three lines over again. This was like the tenth time and all I could do was close the book and sigh. I looked around the library located in University of Rochester and let my head fall on top of my book. Every since Remee left me for his baby mother my life was a wreck. I tried hard to act like nothing had happened. Mostly because I couldn't fall into a dark place and still care for Laya. She was already suffering enough without her daddy around on a daily basis. I wanted to tell him he couldn't see her anymore but, I didn't have the heart to hurt my child. I just allowed him to see her at his mothers since she babysat anyway.

Seeing Miss Layla's number flash across the screen of my phone as it vibrated next to my face I was scared to answer. Lately Laya has been miserable and giving everyone a hard time. "Hello," I answered in a quiet tone.

"Rumor, I know your at school honey but A'Laya is still running a high fever and I think she needs to go in." I frowned, I figured her fever would have broken last night. Gathering my stuff I was out of the building before I could respond.

"I'm on my way, can you please make sure she has on pajama's so I can take her to the ER?" After her grandmother agreed to make sure she was ready I pushed my truck to the max getting out to her house in Pittsford. The minute I walked in the door I knew something was wrong with A'Laya, she was just laying there on the couch. Her glassy eyes not focus on anything.

"I wan't daddy," she cried out as I tried to put her coat on her and then pick her up. This was the part that I hated. I wish he would have just not been involved in her life and this wouldn't have even been a fucking problem.

"Come on we are going to take you to the doctors to get all better." I lifted her in my arms and I wanted to drop her on the ground. She was getting heavy.

"Ma, where she at," Remee called as he flew through the front door. Rolling my eyes I tried to walk by but Laya cried and struggled for his dumb ass. "Rumor, don't get fucked up, I know you hear my kid calling me!"

"And she is sick, her fever is a hundred and four and she needs a doctor. Yo ass aint a doctor." I snapped back.

"I'm coming, let's fucking go." He followed me but I slammed the door in his face. It flew back open like Superman was on the other side. He was scowling, but didn't yell as he walked over and kissed Laya on the head. "Daddy's here, your gonna feel better soon. Get in the back with her, I will drive." I looked up and saw Miss Layla watching us, she shook her head and I respected her enough to listen. This wasn't about me it was about A'Laya. I climbed in the back and held my baby close to me even though she was hot as fuck.

Remee's phone rung bak to back until he finally hit the answer button. "Jayda, what the fuck you want?"

"Remee, I'm in labor, I need you to come to Strong Hospital," she said, her voice filling the vehicle.

"Yo congrats, now get off my line, I'm busy." He ended the call and kept driving. She continued to call causing me to feel guilty as fuck, I didn't want him to miss the birth of his child.

As we pulled up and parked I decided to let him go be with

his family. "Remee, you should go. This isn't as important as your first son being born. We are here, you dropped us. You can go.

"Rumor, why the fuck you gott be hard headed and shit. Give me my shorty so we can get some fucking help." He plucked Laya like she was a feather. "Yo somebody get me a fucking doctor." A nurse came over and then a doctor.

"Ok, we are going to get you into a triage room." They sat us in a small room with a flimsly curtain and a comfy but small bed. I was starting to worry because now Laya wasn't even talking and she had her eyes closed. I knew she needed sleep but it just felt wrong.

"Rem, somethings not right," I said causing him to put us both in his lap and rub my back. His phone rang again and his baby mother sent a nine one one text after.

"Hello," I'm Doctor Newsome. Whats going on with this little one." He asked. I gave him all her symptons and he checked her vitals.

"Remee, go," I pleaded with him. I didn't want him to resent Laya for missing his baby being born.

"Rumor I aint leaving my daughter, stop fucking argu..." He stopped short as Laya started shaking and white foam came out of her mouth.

"Ma'am, sir, please step out of the room now the Doctor ordered. I stood outside crying and praying my child would be ok. Remee who was always in control of everything just stood there looking scared. He wrapped me in his arms and I didn't fight im off, I was too scared to even move. Thoughts of my life without the most important person in it caused me to break down. I wasn't strong enough to lose another child.

"She's coding," someone yelled from behind the curtain before I blacked out.

TO BE CONTINUED...

CPSIA information can be obtained
at www.ICGtesting.com
Printed in the USA
LVHW041945061120
670968LV00003B/489